Negar,

Enjoy!

Love Ijeoma

7/15/12

Tribal Echoes

Restoring Hope

Nkem DenChukwu

Edited by
Chukwueloka Don Okolo

Illustrated by
Chike Kevin Osunkwo

iUniverse, Inc.
Bloomington

Tribal Echoes
Restoring Hope

iUniverse books may be ordered through booksellers or by contacting:

iUniverse
1663 Liberty Drive
Bloomington, IN 47403
www.iuniverse.com
1-800-Authors (1-800-288-4677)

ISBN: 978-1-4697-0941-3 (sc)
ISBN: 978-1-4697-0940-6 (hc)
ISBN: 978-1-4697-0939-0 (e)

Library of Congress Control Number: 2012900063

Printed in the United States of America

iUniverse rev. date: 2/28/2012

DEDICATION

Chinelo Dike, Chinedu Dike, KeleChi Dike, and Chimaobim Dike; my remarkable children: You embrace me wholly, inspire me everyday, and love me tenderly. I love you.

Victoria Chimaluoge DenChukwu; my beautiful and ever-loving mother: Thank you for being my rock. *Nne m oma*, I love you.

Priscilla DenChukwu-Agwu; my loving sister, Kingsley, Eman, Okey and Okwudili DenChukwu; my loving brothers: You all have a place in my heart. Thanks for those special times we share. You have made me better. I love you.

And

In loving memory of my sister:

Obby Francesca DenChukwu-Nweze: My Guardian Angel. You instilled in me all that is good. I know you are resting in the bosom of our Lord. We'll meet again.

FORWARD

"As we navigate through our personal journeys, we often forget the trials and tribulations that have transpired before our Earthly existence. In doing so, we develop a disconnection between our previous bloodline, thus nearly severing the connection with offspring to come.

Being open to new ideas (and not-so-new ones) allows us to re-establish that connection that we so desperately need to truly identify our birth-given royalty. I was delighted to find such rich, authentic ideals and stories in this publication.

What gets overlooked is the transitional period one must experience when moving from one cultural environment to another. The gestures, language barriers, social issues, faux pas, and varying physical appearances are all taken too seriously because of lack of understanding, tolerance, and knowledge.

In a world where we're quick to judge, condemn, or even praise and edify, it's refreshing to read words on a page that exemplify the grass roots effect of common human decency that is not so common anymore.

When you're seen as someone from the "outside," it's imperative that you rekindle with your "insides." You are no stranger to God; therefore you are kept in His good graces…always. And it's those good graces that carry you when you cannot stand; they give you strength in your moment of weakness and provide light in your darkest hour.

This book is heartfelt, eye-opening, and as real as it gets. In a world where change is the only constant, preparing yourself to the best of your ability for life's hills and valleys is your best defense. The vivid and encouraging stories found in these pages will certainly awe you; it will open up a whole new life's perspective for you on the trials that we all endure on all levels. Prepare to shed tears, and shout in joy. You will be immersed in deep thoughts.

Tribal Echoes is certainly a bestseller!"

Erika Gilchrist "The Unstoppable Woman," Chicago, IL. Award-Winning Speaker & Acclaimed Author

"Seldom in the present generation of lettered Igbo parents and pundits, do we find such bold expose of wits and solid determination to sustain the Igbo language and culture through literary work. The biting realities displayed in TRIBAL ECHOES cry out loud for brave ambassadors in rare mold of the author. DenChukwu writes in beautiful punch notes that invite all hands on the deck, for concerted action to save a nation. Chi ndị-Igbo gọzie gị, nwaada."

Isi-Ichie Ben Okpala (Omenanwayo), Houston, Texas.
Author & Educator

AUTHOR'S REMINDER

Nelson Mandela reminds us of the essence of education when he said; "Education is the most powerful weapon which you can use to change the world."

Therefore, if you are a citizen of a country by birth (*Jus Solis*), it does not determine your root. Your bloodline (*Jus Sanguineous*) is your heritage. It is important and necessary to educate yourself about your lineage. You will be amazed at what you will find. This, I know for a fact.

No matter where you were born or live, Culture Matters

I have always been inspired by the differences in culture. In Africa, some regions enjoy close similarities in all aspects of their traditional practices. As a whole, they are similar. But the small differences are generally noted in degrees and finesse in pageantry, and in the particular belief that had been laid down through the ages. The Igbo culture is unique in values. You could tell an Igbo person in a crowded room, even before he opens his mouth. And not just from the way he carries his bags, but from a number of these eclectic superlatives with his notably heavy presence: The foods, the attires, and if his name doesn't tell you something, his music will, as so will his dance routine, and the bragging that follows regarding the traditional marriage ceremonies. However, it is the Igbo names that have the potential to run one through the mill… in a good way. Not only do I love the stories some of the names carry with them, there is also that rich resonance that invokes panache, and then the symbolism present in every chatter, that has the potential to elevate the man or woman who bears it. Hear this: **DIKE A N'AGBALỤ IZU**…

This book is an effort to encourage every race, especially the Igbos, to love the beauty of their native tongue. All languages are unique and beautiful in all of their passages. In as much as we have tried to imbibe or try to adapt into a culture that is not ours, we should strive not to lose the culture and traditions we were born into. That is the threat most cultures and believes face, especially with the Igbos. Our heritage distinguishes us from all others. It is true; where we come from makes each of us inimitable.

ACKNOWLEDGMENTS

"First, I acknowledge the One Spirit who sees me, hears me, and loves me graciously every season; My God. I thank You for the graces in my life: For the gift of life and love, the gift of health, the gift of hope, the gift of laughter, the gift of wisdom, the gift of family, and the gift of true friends. Thank you Father, for simply loving me, inspite of my imperfections…

IkeChukwu Obasi *aka Iyke*:

Thank you for the encouragement and the inspiration. And thank you for cracking me up with your sense of humor.

Chinedu Madubuike *aka Bangkok*:

You are one of my angels on earth. Thank you '*Banky*' for always thinking of me, and considering me.

Christy Ray-Okoye:

My sister, Obby, could not have chosen a more loving best friend than you. Thank you for being you.

Aku Aghazu-Fabusoye:

You hurt when I hurt and smile when I smile. I am thankful that you are my soul sister, and my best friend.

Chinazor Iwuoha-Ikpegbu:

You find ways to keep my hopes alive. They make me richer. Thank you for being my all-weather friend.

Chukwueloka Don Okolo:

My compadre in the arts and a great friend, thank you for so much time.

Dr. Chris Ulasi:

Thank you for your support.

Ugo Sabi-Nweke:

Thank you for your encouraging words. It is great to know that I have a sister next door.

Uju and Sylvan Odobulu:
Thank you for your friendship and support.

Oby Onyeama-DenChukwu, Queen Chukwu-DenChukwu and Mosun Adetola-DenChukwu:
I am glad you are part of my family.

Ugonwa Nweze, Nkiruka Nweze and Chidera Agwu; my nieces:
It feels great knowing that I am in your thoughts. I love you.

Azuka & Roy Chukwu, Yvonne Mbanefo, Dr. Augusta Onwas, Ejike E. Okpa II, Nikki Ajiereen, Adaobi Onyeama, Anthony Ogbo, McDon Ndu, Chike Nweke, Dr. Magdy Rizk, Njide & Wale Adeduntan, Juelle-Ann Daley, Yvonne Chiana, Prince Aboy Aniagu, Buife Nsofor, Jesus Avila, Ifeoma Chukwujindu, Barbi Barkley, Dr. Loretta Mbaduagha, Nnameka Anagbogu, D. Christine Brown, Daniella Cisneros, Chioma Obasi, Ifeoma Opene-Obi, Anthony Igbinovia, Constance Okeke, Doris Ibekwe, Ndubuisi Nebo, Anthonia Okafor, and Olendu Okorafor:
You have each supported me one way or the other. I appreciate you. Thank you.

ND

CONTENTS

About The Book 1

The Color Of My Skin 3

PART ONE
HOW IT ALL BEGAN

1. A NATION OF TONGUES 18
2. THE IGBOS 24
3. TRADITIONAL MARRIAGE IN IGBOLAND . . . 33
4. IGBO CULTURE IN DIASPORA 37

PART TWO
A COLLECTION OF INSPIRATIONAL STORIES

5. EVERYDAY MIRACLE 40
6. A STORY BEHIND A NAME 45
7. THE THIN LINE 48
8. WANNABES 50
9. WHEN HARRY MET AKU. 53
10. CHINELO: THE WILL OF GOD 55
11. IJE: THE JOURNEY 57
12. LIFE: A GRACIOUS GIFT 60
13. DEATH IS NOT THE END... 63

14. THE CRAVING: SWEET AND SOUR 66

15. LOVE: THE JOURNEY OF LIFE 68

16. HOPE, FAITH, AND LOVE 74

17. ALMOST LIKE 'SARAH' 80

18. WHEN THREE BECOMES ONE... 83

19. THE CHAMELEON "OGWUMAGANA" 86

20. 'TO BE OR NOT TO BE...' 90

21. EZIGBO M: MY LOVE 94

22. THE SILENT PRAYER 97

23. AN ANGRY HEART: A RAGING STORM 104

24. PEEK-A-BOO... WHEN THINGS FALL APART . .109

25. BEHIND THE CLOUDS 116

Epilogue 125

Illustrations and Glossaries 127

Igbo/English Glossary 135

English Connotations/Equivalents of Igbo Names 143

Igbo Names And Their Unique Meanings 149

Think About These For A Moment 175

References 176

About The Book

TRIBAL ECHOES is about restoring hope. It is a book about a compelling tribe of people. It chronicles the varying cultures among tribes, especially that exclusive one that belongs to the Igbos of Eastern Nigeria. Among other things, it is a social commentary on a range of issues. The book also details the importance of early childhood education and how one's culture is entwined with it.

As parents, guardians and community leaders, it is therefore imperative that through proper nurturing, our children are aware of their cultural heritage from early childhood. Every parent should embark on this journey to teach their children the ways of their ancestors. The quest at making children culturally aware has its benefits. In the likely event that they are successful, it would come handy in shaping the child, especially that spiritual foundation that always seems to guide certain, if not all behaviors.

Tribal Echoes is about the liberation from the shackles of Colonial conditioning. However, a brief history of Nigeria makes the cut. The customs and traditions of the Igbo nation, their language/dialects, and names, are part of the reason this book was written. Part two of the book is fictional. It is a collection of short stories inspired by the Igbo language and culture.

The Color Of My Skin

It is true that first generation African-American families brought to the new world did not drop from spaceships, they came in slave ships. Somehow, somewhere in time past, many Africans, young and old were abducted from different parts of the beautiful continent of Africa and sold into slavery. They were shipped to the New World called 'America.' Overtime, they became 'African-Americans.'

U.S citizens, including African-Americans, are fortunate to have been born in America. Millions of people from all nationalities dream of coming to America. In almost every case with these immigrants, they hope that someday they would become U.S citizens, or at least, obtain a permanent residency status. They would rather not be tagged 'Aliens,' legal or not!

Every race has its unique and prominent features, values and culture. Africans are distinguished by their diverse nationalities, physical features and inimitable traditions. They vary in beliefs, languages, dialects, tribes, foods, clothing, music, arts, and more. When you see someone from the Horn of Africa, an Ethiopian for example, there is an obvious fact that stands out. Their distinct facial feature is apparent just as it would be with a similar encounter with a Chinese or an Indian.

Pause for a second. Delete all forms of discrimination, all superiority and/or inferiority complex from the frame of your mind. Now, ask yourself: Who is an immigrant in the United States?

Given what we know about American history, this question must exclude the Native Americans. When this question is examined, it could go back to the beginning of time...the time before Christ and even beyond. One generation begets another. This cycle of life or bloodline will continue as long as there is life. It is true to say that the human race is interconnected. The things that connect us are many and will remain eternally unbroken.

In recent genealogical studies, African-Americans have been known to trace their roots to particular tribes in Africa. The same goes with the larger white population, whose roots go back to Europe and Asia. Among African-Americans, the surprising oneness in heritage becomes a given. Every American therefore, with the exception of the Native Americans, is an immigrant.

The African countries with the most connection with mainland African-Americans are Ghana, Cameroon, Kenya, Nigeria, Liberia, and Senegal. There are no surprises whatsoever. Only it is amazing when I see an African-American that clearly resembles someone I know in Nigeria.

Skin color is that unique fabric of oneself that cannot be traded in any marketplace. It is my inheritance, bestowed upon me by nature. Nothing could delete that glaring fact. It is therefore a big part of what makes me stand out.

Before I came to the United States, like many, I had a perception of America. I saw America as heaven here on earth. I admired, and still do, the beauty in their beliefs and the kind of hope that America offers her citizens and immigrants.

My orientation growing up in Nigeria as an Igbo girl was culturally rich. I was nurtured in the Igbo culture, yet exposed to the fullness of the cultural and social images of America. That does not preclude her politics.

American products, her famous and the not-so-famous people, signature way of life, and that accent that is uniquely American, were the driving forces behind the appreciation many of us had. I had hopes for a better life and a brighter future. Ultimately, coming to America seemed like the place to start. So I dreamed of America until it became a reality.

Living in the United States has not been a bed of roses. There have been struggles, not all of which were flagrant. But the bad experiences were complex in nature, and I had soon begun to question a lot of things. And neither was it rare; the struggles of being an African in this vast temperate region. Even in the midst of subtle and not-so subtle discrimination, as practiced by some, the drastic changes in climate had its toll. And then, to be called an 'Alien' in the country of aliens?

But, I did not once take my eyes off the ball. The values I brought with me, sustained me. For one, I had a strong maternal figure in my mother who guided and nurtured me. That did not and could not have goaded me to forget some of those sweet and sour experiences as an African living in America. Some of those experiences have helped in shaping the woman that I am today. And they have continued to energize me, and strengthen my way of thinking.

Some of my bitter-sweet experiences started in the East Bay Area of California. While a student at a community college, I was exposed to people from different nationalities, including African-Americans. Some were very hostile because I had an African accent. Others were unkind and indifferent when they related to me because I did not dress *chic* and/or perhaps did not routinely fix my hair as would a typical African-American female. Not even a French manicure would do to elevate my social status to the level that would be appreciated. I knew that I was different just like everyone else. But I also knew that there was nothing I could've done to change my unique identity in ways that would appease these folks.

My uncut *Africaness* would not allow me to conform. It was no fault of mine. My resources were limited at the time, so I would occasionally wear my brothers' shirts and jackets to school. Swapping clothes with my siblings became the norm for me. But I knew how not to cross the line; I never wore their underwears. However, I was very thankful for those big blessings that came in small boxes.

While going through these experiences, I could hear my mother's voice telling me:

'Nkem my daughter, when you are in an unfamiliar environment, stand on one leg until you've learned somethings about the people. And then you can firmly stand on both feet.'

So, I observed everyone around me. I was subtle in my actions, but sharp in my thoughts.

In the spring of 1995, while waiting for the Physics professor in the laboratory with some of the students, an African-American male student walked up to me. He wanted to chat. I obliged him.

"I like the way you talk. You sound different, in a sexy *kinda* way. It is very appealing." He confessed with aplomb.

He was interested in knowing more about my culture, especially as it pertained to the African woman. He had heard that African women take care of their men. While we were chatting, an African-American female student, Nicole, rudely interrupted our seemingly intense, but interesting conversation. She was doing nothing to conceal her anger. Something had obviously caused her to drift into fits of hysteria. My suspicion was that she had heard me by way of my accent. And clearly in her mind, I was a lesser individual; an African not American enough.

Her sudden outburst wasn't exergerated. She was rolling in absolute meltdown.

"Who do you think you are; Queen of the universe? You think you are all *thaaaat*? All the way from the jungle and the rest of us will have to lose our jobs? You take our men and now you probably want the blouse off my back! *Shiiiit*. What do these American men see in you anyway? Do you think that you are smarter and more cultured? You should pack up, catch the next flight to Kunta Kinte land and leave us the hell alone."

At this time, all eyes were on me...everyone was expecting a stormy reaction from me. But, I was calm, and had a smile on my face.

However, I was not surprised by Nicole's bad behavior because it was not my first time encountering people with such attitude. Malcolm X could not have expressed this better; "Just because a cat has kittens in the oven, that doesn't make them biscuits."

So, I said to myself, 'Welcome to the United States of America.'

I understood that Nicole's unexpected eruption could have been out of ignorance, self-rejection, self-pity, insecurity, culture orientation disability, and intra-group jealousy. I was neither upset nor did I feel degraded.

Based on what had transpired between Nicole and me, I tried to make some sense out of her rude behavior. I decided to find out a little bit more about her. She was born in New York. Her father was African-American and her mother, a Chinese. I was hoping I was wrong about her. But I wasn't. It was obvious that the way she looked on the outside was diametrically opposed to the kind of person she really was.

For me, the disturbing thought was that Nicole neither considered herself a Chinese nor an African. It was clear that she basically saw herself as an American. Nevertheless, I saw the need to educate her and the rest of the class who cared to listen to what being an African meant.

"Do you know your family tree? Ask yourself how you got to be born in America. Do you know who you really are, or who your ancestors were? What does your name mean... if anything? If your skin color is black, do not get confused because you are an African. If you have African blood running in your veins, and you are light-skinned with 'Kinky', Caucasian, or Asian-looking hair, you are an African. If your father is African and your mother is not, that makes you an African. Your country of birth is not the same as your nationality. Where you were born does not necessarily determine who you are. It does not define your root. The distinction is your bloodline! So ask yourself: Who is a true American? Who am I?"

As I spoke, I tried to gauge their expressions and sure enough, Nicole was speechless. I continued with our one-sided conversation by telling her a little more about myself and where I come from. Everyone sat steady, listening attentively. But for Nicole, her earlier outburst had seemingly turned into a valuable lesson for her. She was undoubtedly embarrassed, and didn't know whether she should stay or leave. As a result of this incident, many students became more receptive in their dealings with people from other nations. They also started to appreciate and show openness to cultures that are different from their own.

Contrary to Nicole, **Jawanza**; a Congo name meaning **Dependable**, is not the typical African-American male. His family has always shown an interest in the African culture.

This is from Jawanza:

"Girl, I am an African. I have always considered myself an African, even as I was born and raised in America. Although, I lack the original African values, I am yearning to know everything there is to know about my African heritage. And I intend to find out who I am and where my roots are anchored in the Motherland for as long as it would take me."

Jawanza embraced the true African in him. He hoped that someday, he would marry a blue blood African woman, one born and raised in Africa. To date, he remains one of my dearest friends. He imbibed the nuances in my culture; the language of my people, the clothes, the people, and especially, that gourmet Igbo cuisine he loves so much. His African-American parents are also proud Africans. They taught Jawanza well. He presently lives in Ghana and is married to a Ghanaian woman. In 2009, they were blessed with their first child. A recent conversation with Jawanza revealed that his family finally traced their lineage to the Bamileke tribe of Cameroon.

The excitement in his voice was immeasurable as he described the experience:

"Nkem, when you see me, my father and the people from the Bamileke tribe, you will see the striking resemblances. It is the work of God. I am just grateful."

I could hear it in his voice, the sound of a satisfied soul; the soaring of a lifted spirit that would seem to sing a song: I am home at last! I couldn't be happier for him. He had told me that I was the one reason behind his adventures in Africa. I have since acknowledged his kind words and believe in my heart that God may have used me as an instrument.

In the beginning, many Africans were brought to the American mainland, and sold into slavery. This trade in humans could have dampened the African spirit. And the rest of the world did not fare too well from it, neither. Because of this trade, many lives and lineages were lost, hearts were broken, and families were torn apart.

Many African-Americans are still struggling with their true identity, unsure of who they really are and where their ancestors had come from; the complexities of being an African in the Whiteman's land. The idea itself is strange, and brings with it, a hint of degradation. To call someone born and bred in America an African is a hard pill to swallow for some. Hence, attaching the tag 'American' completes some of them… and justifiably so.

While some African-Americans focused only on the tourist attractions in Africa, others have channeled their interests in knowing the history behind their origin. Many African-Americans who choose not to continue living in the bondage of ignorance are doing something about their situation; they are digging, striving to find their roots. Only they have been marginally successful with these efforts.

The successes include notable African-Americans like Oprah Winfrey who traced her genetic make-up to the Kpelle people of Liberia. Other African-American celebrities that have embarked on this journey to find their African roots include Chris Rock: He discovered his roots to the Udeme people of Cameroon; LeVar Burton, from the TV series, "Roots by Alex Haley" who played the part of Kunta Kinte, has his lineage linked to the Hausa tribe of Nigeria. Bill Cosby, Dr. Maya Angelo, Will Smith, and Toni Morrison could be searching for their roots. Who knows, the race to know could be on full throttle, and people are going back to the source; the cradle of civilization to find out. This is one sure fire way to build the bridge that would keep body and soul together.

On the other hand, many Africans born and raised in Africa are in a struggle to fit into the Western culture. Many would rather prefer to be labeled Americans, even Europeans, as a way of forcing everyone to see them as more urbane.

Back in high school, I met a few girls that, given a chance to get married would have done so for all the wrong reasons. Every one of them would have preferred, and would have loved to marry a Whiteman (an *oyibo*) for one simple reason; to have an *oyibo* baby.

One time, I had a girl say this to me: 'I just want my kids to look different, especially my daughters… you know, just for the hair.' Eventually, she did marry a White-American and had two children by him. Her weird dream was realized; her children had curly hair. It is worth repeating… she married for all the wrong reasons. Apparently, she was also ignorant and battling with self-rejection, insecurity, and culture orientation disability.

Often times, people are roped inadequate in their self-imposed battles as they struggle to become something that they are not. It becomes a swirling, recoiling nightmare, a bad journey that could, if not restricted, destroy that individual. Eventually, they lose themselves. To bleach your way out of your blackness, and to talk virtually without one's African accent, does not change who you are. I know for a fact that some Africans love it when they seem to have lost a sizeable drone in the way they originally sounded before coming to America. Maybe these Africans sound more polished than others because they have been outside their native country for so long. But still, it does not change who they are.

I am not surprised when people ask me; 'Where are you from? I hear an accent.'

Naturally, I smile and would be quick to tell them that I am Igbo. Yet, some people are offended when told that they have an accent. It is clear why that is so. I do love the fact that I have an accent. An accent distinguishes me from another; that is part of what makes me unique.

Most African children born in the United States tend to have the American accent. It is the other part of their heritage. Even though they have dual citizenship, it is still every parent's responsibility to make sure their children know and understand their roots. That should keep them grounded where their appetites are whetted enough to embrace their other heritage as Africans and not just as African-Americans.

A Nigerian-American teenager had an interesting conversation with another Nigerian teenager who was born in Nigeria. After their brief chat, the teenager in Nigeria was sad and was to an extent, jealous of the Nigerian-American teenager. She would give anything to sound like the other teenager. The disappointing thing these days is that many African-born children and those born outside of Africa are not properly educated in their native tongues. The reason for this cultural shortcoming is because their parents also suffer from Western cultural superiority complex. This is a trend, and may very well be the start of the terrible things to come; *the extinction of the Igbo way of life, her customs, and traditions.*

One wonders why parents would choose to suppress their native language in lieu of a foreign one. 'My children can understand my native language, but they cannot speak it.' That's how it starts! Or, 'My children can neither understand my native language nor speak it.' That clearly stokes it! Many parents sing this like a song, and say it with such pride. Therefore, it is not surprising that children, especially the ones born and raised in Nigeria are unable to communicate in their mother tongue.

Picture this for a second: An Igbo girl born of Igbo parents, in Lagos, Nigeria…therefore, she is fluent in Yourba. Her native tongue; Igbo language, becomes a foreign language. If I must say, it is ridiculous and a shame!

If the trend is not reversed, we could lose a big part of who we are. If only parents would take the time to teach their children, their efforts should payoff; the kids would, inadvertently learn to live and preserve that which has been given to them. They would most likely pass this on to the next generation. That is how culture survives; how traditions and customs are preserved among people.

However, some Africans that were born in America prefer to be tagged wholesomely American. Many of them have gotten used to saying this tiresome maxim;

"I am an American, but my parents are Africans."

A typical American is inclined to say; "I am originally from San Francisco and my parents are from North Carolina," even when he/she is uncertain where he/she is originally from. Just because you were born in San Francisco, New york, Chicago, or San Antonio, it does not mean you are originally from there. Or just because you and/or your family relocated from one city/state/country to another, lived in that specific area for many years and acquired the local accent, still does not mean that it is where you are from. Your root simply means where you are originally from. It must lead to your parents first, and carried over to your grandparents and so on. That is your family tree. Period!

I can appreciate it when a child born of African parents in the United States says for instance, "I am a Nigerian-American" rather than saying, "I am an American." It makes me wonder where their African heritage fits in. This cycle of ignorance has continued from one generation to another and it needs to be broken.

While in-flight traveling from the State of Maryland, I was sitting next to a 21 year old college student named Vanessa. When I ended my phone conversation in my native language, her face had lit up with a smile so electrifying that it was frozen in place. I could hear the question she had for me even before she had the opportunity to ask it.

"Hi. Are you Ibo?" Vanessa asked, the smile still riding piggy-back. I humbly responded, also with a smile. "Yes, I'm Igbo, born and raised in *Naija* (Nigeria)."

"I was born and raised in Dallas, Texas," she said warmly, the smile widening. "I am Ibo too, I mean Igbo," she continued, as if she had seen some doubt in my mind. In the same breath, she stopped momentarily to rewrite the pride her face bore. "I just wish I could speak the language."

I told her that wishing and doing are two different things. When you think and do, you have results; good or bad. Her eyes shifted from me to the window in shame. Even though Vanessa was born and raised in America, she is one of the very few young Nigerian-Americans that introduces herself in this very appropriate manner. Since that day, we have stayed in touch, and I have become her extemporaneous mentor in all matters cultural.

"I cannot speak the Igbo language because my parents, who are also Igbos, did not teach my siblings and me the language. They rarely spoke to us in Igbo when we were kids. I understand bits and pieces of it when mixed with the English language."

Vannesa had expressed this to me in very subtle tone.

She may sound American, but every inch of her being reflects that of an Igbo woman, Adaeze; the princess. Nevertheless, she loves the Igbo language and the Igbo culture. She enjoys her summer visits to Nigeria. It is not too late for her to learn and grasp the language because she is eager to learn it. She gets excited each time I say something to her in Igbo.

Vanessa expressed to me her disappointment that Nigerian-Americans, young adults especially, those that have never visited Nigeria, most often than not, do not know how to speak the language of their parents. "Clearly, they have lost a sense of their culture that can only be regained most times by visiting Nigeria. I think the ones living in Nigeria have more respect for the elders to an extent. They also put greater emphasis on education. However, once they come to America, they tend to lose sight of what is important and try to fit into the American culture. Everyone wants to fit in," she lamented.

Although, not everybody wants to fit in, but most times, many do hope that they could. I agree with Vanessa. This is about culture and tradition. No matter where you were born or where you live, culture should matter. There is nothing wrong with embracing a culture that is not yours. However, one should not have to lose the values they were born into in an effort to absorb that which is foreign.

The older generations of immigrant Africans have a better handle on who they are. They are a lot better at maintaining their *Africanness;* their values and cultures. The so-called Digital Natives; the new generations of African immigrants are not so good at maintaining their identity. Furthermore, they are slow, and sometimes fail altogether in raising their children in that proper manner the African culture and traditions demand.

The error is almost irreversible after a certain age in any child's life. Children born to these parents find it harder to learn to speak the language of their ancestors. They follow that notorious path to nowhere, because they are no longer teachable. These children would wallow emptily in the dark, if and when they go searching for their roots. During the search, they are usually in the throes of a mild shiver; there is no clarity in their approach, and the values that should have taken center stage, and should have led the search are undoubtedly misplaced.

When I speak in my native tongue; the Igbo language, I love it and I am proud. I speak it to my children. Sometimes they understand it and most times, sadly enough they do not! My kids are definitely aware of the fact that they are Igbos; not because of the food they eat. They know the language I speak sounds foreign to a certain degree. I am one of many parents guilty of not teaching her children their mother's tongue early. Granted they were born and raised in the States and have not yet visited Nigeria, they know where they are originally from. They understand and appreciate the meanings of their names and who they are. Now, I am on a mission. When it's noisy in my home, I tell my kids to speak in their mother tongue. And all of a sudden, the house is quiet. This is not funny, but it works. It makes them want to learn the language of their mother.

It is not all about language. Those people that tend to love the Western culture and then try to assimilate it often times would not completely fit into that new culture they have adopted. No matter how much people yearn for something new to propagate their ego and false social well-being, something that they do not genetically own, they'd fail, and then eventually fall face down in ignominy. For instance, the skin color black can never be bought or exchanged. When one tampers with this unique color, in an attempt to make it lighter, it is ruined and cannot be rejuvenated to its original state. There is no substitute for being black because black is just black, unique and yes, beautiful.

To be black is to be from a unique heritage. To love and be proud of who you are, regardless of your ethnicity or nationality is everything. When one attempts to look, sound, and act like another, in an effort to fit into a profile, it does not change who you truly are. All people are made in the image of God. We are different, yet we share similarities. If you are black, but speak the language that is not yours, and not your mother tongue, you are still black. It is that simple.

There is Africa in every black person.

"Our deepest fear is not that we are inadequate. Our deepest fear is that we are powerful beyond measure. It is our light, not our darkness that frightens us most. We ask ourselves, 'Who am I to be brilliant, gorgeous, talented, and famous?' Actually, who are you not to be? You are a child of God. Your playing small does not serve the world. There is nothing enlightened about shrinking so that people won't feel insecure around you.

We were born to make manifest the glory of God that is within us. It's not just in some of us; it's in all of us. And when we let our own light shine, we unconsciously give other people permission to do the same. As we are liberated from our own fear, our presence automatically liberates others." Maryanne Williamson, 'Our Deepest Fear.'

As we try to understand our heritage, we can also see a glimpse of how history can help us identify who we are. Malcolm X once stated: "You have to have knowledge of history no matter what you are going to do; anything you undertake, you have to have knowledge of history in order to be successful in it. The thing that has made the so-called Negro in America fail, more than any other thing, is your, my, lack of knowledge concerning history." In essence, history is paramount in explaining a person's past and a purposeful future.

Culture is the essence of human existence and should be constantly expressed in our development. Culture is the very flavor that determines where we all come from; it reminds us where we are, and sustains us until we get to where we are going. Human race creates events therefore, histories are made. One does not have to go where history happened to learn from it. We need to remember that history cannot be denied, just like our heritage.

Change is good. It is meant to strengthen us. After all, it is 'the only constant thing in life.' It is not meant to weaken us, or for us to forget who we are, and who we aspire to be. When you don't fight change, and you take your heritage along with you, then you would have arrived.

Our fore-fathers and our fathers may have failed to teach us Africans and African-Americans about who we truly are. If we continue to thread on the same path of ignorance and fear of the unknown, the digital natives; the new generation, will continue to thread on the same path. It is up to me, you and all of us, to teach ourselves, our children, grandchildren, as well as our neighbors who we are and not who we are trying to be. In this way, we can be proud and smile, while saying, 'My name is... I am originally from...' That would be a start.

Black is what I am and not what I am trying to be. Black is simply Africa and then African. Gracious? Yes, and sustaining as far as heritage goes. "I am an American, but my parents are Africans." I stand to correct this notion each time I hear it. But, who is listening?

My name is Nkem DenChukwu. I was born and raised in the Igbo tribe of Nigeria, in West Africa.

BE 100% ORGANIC.

BE PROUD OF YOUR HERITAGE,

BECAUSE THAT IS WHO YOU ARE

PART ONE
HOW IT ALL BEGAN

Nigeria is the most populous country in Africa. The country is blessed with many natural resources of which crude oil is the biggest source of her foreign exchange. The three main ethnic groups are the Hausas, Igbos and Yorubas. Each tribe is unique in tradition with of course, significant cultural differences. Colonized by the British, the English language is the main form of communication. There are two dorminant religions in this country of over 150 million people: Christains and Muslims. Only a small minority of the population still practices other forms of traditional religion.

MAJOR ETHNIC GROUPS, LANGUAGES AND DIALECTS

The Hausas are mainly located in the northern parts of Nigeria. The tribe is an integration of the Songhai Empire; people who share the same way of life. The Hausaland was created as a predominatly Muslim nation. Today, they remain the majority group in the nation. It is not clear if that is a fact. But, who is arguing? Their language is Hausa.

The Yorubas occupy the Oduduwa land, located in southwestern region of Nigeria. History reveals that the ancient Yorubas believed in Oduduwa as a diety almost in parity with Jesus Christ. They are one of the ethnic groups in Africa whose cultural heritage and legacy are well documented in the Americas. Their language is Yoruba.

One will find the Igbos mainly in the southeastern region of Nigeria. They are one of the largest and most influential ethnic groups in Nigeria. Six years after the British left Nigeria, the Igbos declared Igbo nation, calling it the 'State of Biafra.' This declaration inadvertently led to a civil war that lasted for 36 months. The Igbos are mainly Christians with a negligible few still holding on to traditional practices. The language of the Igbos is called **Asụsụ Igbo**. However, the English language serves as a medium of communication nationwide. But, an English copulation of certain native slangs and proper words known as BROKEN or PIDGIN ENGLISH is commonly used.

ASỤSỤ IGBO

The Igbo language is a tonal language, beautiful in its excerpts and spoken by over 25 million people. The syllable of each word is pitched high or low in relation to one another. Each word has a distinctive tone to it.

However, almost every name in the Igbo language has a measure of great significance. Most Igbo names are never lost in their translation because of their unique meanings. Some of the names have haunting stories attached to them. A great many of the Igbo names are linked to the existence of God: For example, **Chukwueloka/Olisaeloka/Chinelo (The Will of God)**. This is because the Igbos are predominantly Christians. The vast ranging stories and the meanings behind these names are the reasons these native names are uncommoningly beautiful.

THE DIGITAL NATIVES AND LANGUAGE

Many African parents do not instill in their children the beauty of their native language, and to a larger extent, their cultural heritage. Rather, most parents choose to focus on borrowed culture, especially that of the Western/European way of life. No one is sure why some are motivated to do this. The most likely explanation had to be dislike for oneself and abject ignorance.

In many African households, the English language is the chosen and preferred language. As it is used day after day, our generation and the next generation coming are rinsed clean of all essential parts of their heritage. In many families, the unspoken rules are in full burst of fervor in an effort to be branded civilized and sophisticated. They lose track of what is important in their lives and adopt the Whiteman's (***Oyibo/Bekee***) way of life.

In a world where everything seems to be changing rapidly and technological influences are visible in almost everything imaginable, culture still remains an integral aspect of life. Technology may be changing the world, but culture remains supreme and will be the sole propagator of all traditional values that truly define who we are. The newer generations are greatly influenced by the Western cultures thereby making them DIGITAL NATIVES.

In the end, it is imperative that we embrace these tribal echoes because they hold the real essence of our heritage.

This book primarily focuses on events inspired by the Igbo culture and language.

CHAPTER 1
A NATION OF TONGUES

Nigeria, officially known as the Federal Republic of Nigeria comprises of thirty-seven States including its Federal Capital Territory (FCT), Abuja. The country is located in West Africa and shares land boundaries with Chad and Cameroon in the east, the Republic of Benin in the west and Niger in the north. Nigeria's coast in the south is the Gulf of Guinea on the Atlantic Ocean. The name Nigeria was said to be originated from the Niger River.

The country's culture is seen through various works of art like dance, food, literature, music, language, folktale and more. According to archaeological findings, Nigerian descendants and her artifacts boast of an extensively rich history. The earliest discoveries date as far back as 9000 BC. Some of these findings include the Nok culture (Terracotta figures, and the first recorded use of iron as a tool). The Noks lived north of the Benue River from 500 BC to 200 AD.

However, the Iron Age has been attributed to the civilization of the Republic of Sudan and to the North African nation of Carthage. Nigeria's arts and crafts are varied and unique. Most of Nigeria's priced works of art are proudly displayed in Museums the world over (Pottery, ceramics, textiles, bronze, brass etc).

According to the 2008 census report, Nigeria is the most populous country in Africa. It is also considered to be the eighth most populous in the world with 151,212,254 people. Her people are mostly of the black race. The country is blessed with as many natural resources as you would find in a fruit bowl. But, the one most associated with Nigeria is crude oil.

Nigeria is a multilingual nation. It comprises of over 250 ethnic groups, and languages, with diversified cultural and religious backgrounds. The diversity makes her unique. The three largest and most influential ethnic groups are the Hausa (North), Igbo (Southeast) and Yoruba (Southwest). Other ethinc groups are Itsekiri (Niger Delta), Urhobo (Niger Delta), Ijaw (Niger Delta), Ibibio (Niger Delta), Tiv (Middle-belt), Nupe (Middle-belt), Kanuri (North), Efik (South-south), Edo (South-south) and Fulani (North), to mention a few.

In this nation of tongues, the English language serves as a medium of communication. However, an English derivative known as BROKEN or PIDGIN ENGLISH was created by the people as a simpler, much more stylistic substitute to the Whiteman's language. It is so largely spoken, it is considered by many as the only real alternative form of communication in Nigeria. However, no tribe is excluded from the use of Pidgin English. It has been rumored that Nigeria could adopt Pidgin English as an official form of communication between tribes.

Though the English language was forced on Nigerians, the older generations of Nigerians speak in their native tongue because it is the language they were raised in. But, there is a problem: There are those that were born in Nigeria, and to a larger extent, those of them that were born and raised outside of Nigeria, that are not versed in their native language. The result is that they have become unfathomably alienated from the language they inherited. It gets worse: A good many of them would never achieve true mastery in the new mode of communication they had chosen to embrace.

There are two major religious groups: Muslims and Christians. Only a small minority of the population practices other forms of traditional religion.

Nigeria was under the British Colonial rule until October 1, 1960 when she became an Independent Nation. The three dorminant regions amalgamated were the Northern, Western and Eastern land masses. The majority of the population resides in the urban areas. After her independence a fourth region; the Mid-West was carved out of the existing regions of the south. In 1963, Nigeria became a Republic even though it was plagued by power struggles among the ethnic groups.

The Nigerian currency is expressed in Naira (N) and the coin is in kobo (k). 100k is equal to one naira (N1). The currency denominations are N5, N10, N20, N50, N100, N200, N500 and N1, 000. The coins are in denominations of 10k, 25k, 50k and N1 coin.

Since her independence, Nigeria's economy has been unstable and on *life-support.* It stems from one socio-political crisis to another. Her existence has been linked to ineffective leadership. It operates a Presidential System of Government with a National Assembly comprising the Senate and the House of Representatives. Nigeria runs a three-tier System of Government; the Federal, State and Local Governments. Nevertheless, with the 2011 Presidential election, many Nigerians and the rest of the world hope they would see positive changes especially, in the leadership and economic arenas.

Nigeria has two well-defined seasons; the rainy season (**Udu mmiri**) which starts from the month of April and ends through the month of October, and the dry season (**Ọkọchi/ Ụgụrụ**) starts from November through March. The overall temperature is usually high except in the cities of Jos, Mambila and Obudu in Plateau State where the temperature is relatively cool all year round. However, the high temperature is never uniform from coast to coast and it varies as one travels inland going from the semi-arid lands to the fringes of the Sahara.

The southeastern region of Nigeria is the rainforest belt. In this region, you will find the Igbos.

The institutions of higher learning in science, engineering and management premiered as the first generation Federal Universities. The University of Nigeria; Nsukka, University of Ibadan, University of Lagos and Ahmadu Bello University; Zaria are the first institutions of higher learning. Despite the mass exodus in Nigeria, the country has maintained its identity and has made some changes in a desperate bid to retain its diverse cultural fingerprints and traditions. It boasts of great tourist attractions known to the world. Some of these rare sites have been in existence for ages and have acquired significant recognition. It is true that without tourism, some of these attractions would not have achieved national prominence.

Most people are still unaware of the existence of some of these places. It has always been up to the indigenes to publicize, by word of mouth, those local attractions that have not attained national fame. The Nigeria Government should be in a race to document these places and market them to the rest of the world.

Nigeria attracts local and foreign investors, explorers and tourists to her soil because of her potential as a great trading outpost. Tourist attractions in the Western region of Nigeria include Olumo Rock in

Abeokuta, the palaces of Oni of Ife and Alafin of Oyo; the Ogbunike Cave in Anambra State, the Obudu Cattle Ranch in Cross River State, Yankari Games Reserve in the Emirate of Kano and the Tinapa Resort in Calabar of Cross-River State.

However, most media reports have not cared so much about Africa proper. What this means is that the greater Africa, like the sub-regions, hinterlands, the nooks and cranies are never parts of front line news. As a consequence, the beauty of Africa was told in the back pages of low level news outlets. The media has also continued to focus on the not-so-appealing stories and images of Africa as a country instead of as a continent. As a consequence too, and just like most African Nations, Nigeria has suffered immeasurably because of this undercoverage. Only Statesmen and nation builders are now attempting to reconstruct the storylines in the hope of telling much more compelling narratives to the rest of the civilized world.

One should not totally judge a book by its cover until one has read the book. Nigeria's credibility has been smudged by her own people; by mostly individuals with no moral compass. They would, under no circumstance, stop to think about the damage they stand to inflict on their country. If there is money to be made, the consequences of their actions notwithstanding, these leeches would carry on with their schemes. The four-one-niners (419-ners; Con artists as they are called) are Nigeria's worst nightmares.

The local kidnappers are a much greater pain. It is ironic that they would remain eternally fixtured on street corners and/or at the bottom of the compost pit, with no real attempts made to rein them in.

However, one bad apple should not spoil a whole bunch. Or could it? The incompetent leadership in Nigeria has contributed to a deteriorating and disheartening social and economic infrastructure. In addition, it has continued to jeopardize the lives and welfare of her citizens, especially with the not-so-distinguishable middle-class and the poor. In spite of it all, Nigeria is rich in culture and natural resources. There are shades of hope still in the offing; discernible whiffs of integrity are still palpable to keep the country's body and soul together a little while longer. Maybe someday, a great stable nation will emerge from this chaos, only she has a lot of work to do if she was to clean up her own mess.

BIAFRA

The Igbos in their quest for a separate State inadvertently put Biafra on the map. With the Igbos, the Biafra nation was an attempt by the leaders of her people to carve out a nation state of their own from the republic of Nigeria. Known as the Secessionist State, the Igbos led by the Late Lieutenant-Colonel Odumegwu Ojukwu, declared the State of Biafra as a way of settling the intra-cultural conflict in Northern Nigeria. In a civil strife, the Muslim north killed the Igbos living on their land.

In 1967, when the killings continued, the Igbos saw a way out of their demise and took it. The Nigerian-Biafran War, also known as the Nigerian Civil War, started thereafter. The Nigerian Government had no other choice, but to wage the war that would reunite the nation.

During the civil war, the invading armies of Nigeria committed many atrocities against the Igbos. The government of Nigeria used starvation as weapons of war. The civil war claimed the lives of hundreds of thousands of Igbos (Biafrans). By the end of the conflict, which lasted for 36 months (from July 6th, 1967 to January 12th, 1970), nearly a million people had lost their lives on the Biafran side.

The Secession the Igbos once believed was their ticket to Statehood was crushed. The victorious Nigerians saw the secessionist Biafrans as rebels without any real cause. The Force marshaled to bring the Eastern Region back under the control of the Central Government was led by ironically, a Christain; General Yakubu Gowon. And, the "Land of the Rising Sun" was no more, and the once budding tribute that was the Biafran's national anthem died in its cradle.

HOME AND ABROAD

The Hausa tribe purportedly has a population of 30 to 35 million. The Igbo tribe is estimated at 25 million. While the Yoruba nation is estimated at about 30 million people. Today, millions of ethnic Nigerians reside outside the country and they do this for many different reasons of which education is one. The search for new opportunities is another. Vacation, child bearing, health or wellness reasons and a host of others are why many Nigerians seek for greener pastures. The estimate of Nigerians living in the United Kingdom is 200,000 to 500,000. The majority of this population comes from the Yoruba tribe. Canada and Spain have large groups of Nigerians too as do many other countries. More than 1,600,000 (One million six hundred thousand) Nigerians reside in the United States. The United States Census Board estimated that the overall population of Nigeria could reach up to 264 million by the year 2050. If that happens, then Nigeria will be the 8th most populous country in the world.

It would be safe to say that the United States of America is home away from home for many Nigerians. In the United States, the Igbos have the largest number of ethnic Nigerians. The cities of Houston and Dallas in Texas, the States of Maryland and New York, the city of Atlanta in Georgia, the cities of Los Angeles and Oakland in California, have great numbers of Nigerians.

Even as many Nigerians reside outside their Motherland, some try not to forget their heritage and where they come from. The diversity of customs, languages and traditions among the ethnic Nigerians living in these adopted homelands, gives the host countries unique cultural tapestry. Culture is expressed through art, dance, literature, music, language, folklore, and foods. It is from among these that the host nations also benefit immeasurably.

CHAPTER 2
THE IGBOS

In Igboland, the language is known as **Asụsụ Igbo** and the people are known as the **Igbos**, and not the **Ibos** like many misconstrue. The Igbo custom is unique. And it is particularly unique because her practioners do so with fervor, blending its finer nuances and the otherwise complex items into an ester of wholesomeness. It is this phenomenom that gives the Igbo culture/customs that buoyant, but brittle edge so loved by many. Take the Igbo attires, traditional marriage rites, music and dance, the language, names and foods for example, and you'll begin to appreciate the greatness of a people. These are what define an Igbo person, even from a distance. Take the New Yam Festival, and the masquerades that add pomp and pageantry to the festivities, and you would have a fiesta to equal that made popular by Bossa Nova practioners in Brazil. The Igbo culture appeals to almost everyone who comes across it. Well, it is the welcoming mat it has spread over a large expanse of other tribal lands. In other words, it accommodates other cultures and customs as a way of propagating her unique attributes.

However, as much as the culture is admired and appreciated, there are parts of it that are not acceptable by some. Idolatry, rituals and polygamy are frowned upon by Christains. But that shouldn't take away from the Igbo man's methods and standards. The Christains know how not to create inter-tribal and intra-cultural feud between brothers.

But one thing remains a thorn in the flesh to both Christains and the practioners of native beliefs; the continued practice of referring to some people of the Igbo extraction as "**Osu** (Outcast) and **Ohu** (Slave)." This belief is as old as humanity itself, and it has remained glued to the Igbo psyche. These people are believed to have been defiled through either a lineage in their ancestry that had been branded as slaves, or were sacrificed to a diety. Because of that, they are not totally assimilated to the general population of the Igbos. It doesn't end there: They are vehemently isolated. Anyone from these 'cursed' families is prohibited from marrying from among the so-called free families.

The Igbo language is spoken in the eastern States of **Abia**, **Anambra**, **Delta**, **Ebonyi**, **Enugu** and **Imo**. The language is also a form of communication used in trade, commerce and in media communication in these states.

The Igbos have an Igbo calendar. The Igbo calendar has four market days in a four-day market cycle, instead of the regular seven-day week. Each village is identified by a specific market day to allow for a fair market share. For instance, a trader has the opportunity to buy and sell goods and services on a market day not assigned to his village.

In Igbo language, '**izu**' is known as the week; the four market days. The days of the week are known as **Eke, Orie, Afọ,** and **Nkwọ**. They are the basic measurements of the Igbo calendar. To say, 'this week' in Igbo would be **izu ụka**. Each market day must pass twice to make up an an **izu**.

The stories behind the four-day market week are varied, but impressive. One of the stories was about a wealthy Igbo man who had eight sons. He named each son an Igbo name that ended with the four market days; Eke, Orie, Afọ and Nkwọ. When the sons became men, each of them inherited from their father, a portion of land some distance from each other.

Family is the core foundation in the Igbo community. Igbo people are bred to strengthen the family structure. They are thought to appreciate it, nurture it, as a means of propagating the only viable entity that binds every family. This practice has tentacles; an extended family idea that adds proportion to the single family unit.

Igwebụike; 'There is strength in unity,' has always been the force behind each family's survival. Remember the wealthy Igbo man with the eight sons in the story? Well, he instilled the concept of unity in his sons to keep his family together. To keep this value alive, the sons added to it by using the market days as family meeting days.

In the old days, a child was named after a market day to denote the day on which he or she was born. For instance, a male child's first name and family name ascribed to any of the market days mentioned above would say thus: **Okeke, Nweke, Okereke, Nwafọ, Okafọ, Nwankwọ,**

Okoronkwọ, Okonkwọ, Nworie and **Okorie.** These are the commonly used names. The female child's first name always has a different sound to it… completely different from that of a male. They may have the same representation. Names like **Mgbeke, Mgbafọ, Mgbọnkwọ,** and **Mgborie** although frowned at, were often used.

Today's generation; THE DIGITAL NATIVES, do not use any of these names as their first names. The names are old fashioned and considered stale; again, they are frowned at and have always been used as parodies. Simply put, these names are considered primitive.

Language is part of everyone's heritage. The Igbo language has syllables that are pitched high and/or low in relation to one another. Each word has a distinctive tone to it. Not so much has been written in the Igbo language. Some prominent Igbo writers wrote and ascribed mostly in the English language and not in the Igbo language. Though the Igbo language is taught in Elementary and Secondary schools, however, many middle class Igbos would rather communicate in English language in their households. This practice has placed the Igbo language under siege; it could most likely be lost forever… dead, somewhere inside the next one hundred years.

For this reason, it is the responsibility of every Igbo person to do whatever it would take to assure that the Igbo language never dies. The chance of this happening is looming, and could very well happen.

Practice does make perfect… well, at least, it does improve one's proficiency in any learned art form. The hardest language could be learned when practiced with discipline and consistency. If the English language is not a person's mother tongue, the native language should therefore be the largest part of one's childhood orientation. Speaking or writing a different language identifies one as a member of that group.

The Igbo language has 20 or more dialects. It is said that in 1972, a standard Igbo language dialect was developed based on two Igbo regions' use of syllabic tone: **Owerri** and **Ụmụahia** in Imo State, to ease communication debacles amongst the Igbos. This dialect was adopted, and it is still used in schools. For instance, to ask the question; **How are you?** In Central Igbo, it would be; **"kedụ?"** as opposed to saying **"Kee otu idi?"** or **"Olee otu imere?"**

Furthermore, the language is not always translated in the English language the way it is literally spoken or written. Sometimes, in an attempt to translate the Igbo language into English, there are the usual ups and downs. Almost in every situation, the meaning is lost in some attempts.

Worst of it, the gist is muddled, and could very well signify something else. Here's an example: the name **Ahamefule** means **One's lineage should not be lost.** However, the literal meaning is: **My name should not be lost**.

The Igbo language is flavored with her eclectic riches and reaches. Inside each dialect are discernible shades and symmetery. The Igbo person is painfully loyal to that unique dialect that is his or hers, and would not always accept the newer versions of a language he/she had already fallen in love with. Making this shift is not always an easy thing to accomplish.

THE IGBO LANGUAGE ALPHABETS (See illustration)

The Igbo alphabets have thirty-six alphabets similar to the Roman Script. It was noted that the Ọnwụ Orthography is the official Igbo alphabet guide. The language has eight vowels, thirty consonants, and two distinctive tones. The eight vowels are called **Udaume**:

a e i ị o ọ u ụ

The use of double articulations or diphtongues (example: ch, kp, gw, and gb) in the consonant system is the defining feature of the Igbo sound system. Each vowel has high and low tones, low and high tones, high and high or low and low tones.

When these tones are combined in a variety of complex ways, sometimes, each tone changes in tonal melody. The three syllable types are shown in the syllabic nasal, vowel, and consonant-vowel sequences.

A typical example of high and low tones in the vowels: A homonym: **Akwa; an Igbo word.**

Akwa means:

Akwa = Cry (High/High)
Akwa = Egg (High/Low)
Akwa = Cloth (Low/High)
Akwa = Bed (Low/Low)

You should try saying the sentence below fast without pausing: TONGUE TWISTER:

Nwata na-akwa akwa, i na-akwa akwa na okụkọ yịrị akwa na-elu akwa ịkwara akwa, di na-elu akwa?

Literal English Translation: **The child that is crying, are you crying because a hen laid an egg on the clothes you sewed, that are on top of the bed?**

A second example:

Egbe (Igbo word):

Egbe (High/Low) = Gun
Egbe (Low/High) = Eagle

E ji m egbe were gbagbuo egbe: English Translation: **I used a gun to shoot an eagle.**

THE BIRTH OF A HERITAGE

The birth of a child is part of God's plan and the reason He said that the world should go on. *The birth of a child is the birth of a heritage.* It is the continuation of the family tree. God said in Genesis 1, verses 27 to 28, "... go into the world and multiply."

Life begins with time itself. And it evolves as time evolves. When a child is born, the journey of life begins, and it is filled with hopes and dreams. No doubt, childhood orientation plays a major role in the early stages of life. If the pattern remains unbroken, that child's development stays unhindered through adulthood. Human development is a complex, infinite process. Only in situations of cerebral decay would the process slow down. Even at that, any small amount of intervention would jump-start, however minimal, the learning process again. In truth, human development never ceases, and would continue until death.

Children are priceless gifts from God

WHAT'S IN A NAME?

Do you ever wonder who you would have been without your name? Your name tells the rest of the world who you are. Naming a child is the patch of true identity. And in the course of the child's growth, nothing else could fashion his attitude, mold his behavior, however subtle, as the name he was given. But a great effort from the child would be required to maintain the trajectory of his origin, if it were to remain unchanged.

In many parts of Nigeria, especially in Igboland, naming a child is greatly festive. The naming ceremony is an occasion that is celebrated. Family and friends are invited to feast. Dance is thrown in, and the erstwhile simple gathering would usually morph into a fiesta of thanksgiving to God for the blessings the family had received.

A child may be given several names that are not included in his birth certificate. These other attributes are usually names given to the child by his distant relatives, one blood or two removed from him. The names are usually imitative of his ancestors, and sometimes, depending on circumstances of birth and delivery, they are so named to mark significant events that had passed.

Historically, the head of a family names the child. In the old days, and to an extent, in today's family, it is the man's place to name the child. Women don't generally get this role. But there are situations that allow a woman to do so. They are rare, but they do exist.

When the Missionaries landed, things began to change, and the changes were drastic. Under the Whiteman's supervision, families were forced to give their children the so-called Christain names, as a way of pacifying the Colonialists and their Christain ways.

Again, the paradigm has shifted: Both parents can now decide on the name/s to be given before or when their child is born. However, the new generations of Igbos are listening to a different drummer; their choices of names are foreign, and lack proper sense and originality. All hope is not dead however, because, the older generations of Igbos are determined to follow the traditional ways of naming their children.

Others whose surnames are traditional Igbo names have changed their names to their fathers' English first names as opposed to bearing their surnames that have been in their families for generations. For instance, **Chukwuemeka Okonkwo, son of David Okonkwo now feels the need to be known as Chukwuemeka David instead. Or, he would choose to drop his Igbo first name, Chukwuemeka, for his Christain name, Michael. Now, his legal name becomes Michael David**.

Some Igbos have changed, and/or rewritten their names into unnecessary nomenclatures, in order to be more embraceable. Well, maybe more marketable. All the name changes are done in an effort to cuddle the Western culture.

The first son in a family always has a significant role to play. Whether he lives up to the role and actually plays it is another thing. But generally, all first born males are standby father representatives. They are there, not just to keep the family tree alive, but also to certify that the practices that had kept the family's life intact didn't die on their watch. So, at any given time, customs and traditions that are passed on from one generation to another have a great chance of surviving, even with the little shifts in translation. Some Igbos, especially the older generations, believe that a female child is the path to all riches; a daughter who marries should bring a measure of wealth to the family she is leaving behind. It is not always true, but the hope of that happening has never waned.

In Igboland, before the Europeans came, a child's first name is usually the given name. All others could follow. Names are thrown in to ascertain lineages from both family trees. There are those that are latched on, because the child looked a certain way; maybe the child has particular idiosyncracies of laughter, or what have you. Some names are earned because the child has the bearing of renowned past warriors. And until the child comes into adulthood, he does not take chieftaincy titled names. But with the advent of the Whiteman, the onetime pristine branding of true identities got sullied.

Most Baptismal and Confirmation names are usually English-based, Latin or French derivatives. But lately, some Christain names are purely Igbo-based. On the other hand, the younger generations name their children without following the traditional naming pattern. Instead, they have chosen to modernize their names into slick-sounding monikers. As a consequence, the root meanings in these names are misinterpreted and/ or completely lost. For instance, names like **Chimamanda** is changed or shortened to Amanda, **Sọmadina** to Dina, **Chinelo** to Nelo or Nelly, **Nkiruka** to Nikki, **Nkem** to Kem or Myne, **Kanene** to Kanii, **Nkemdilim** to Kimberly, **KeleChi** to Kelly, and **KọbeluChukwu** or **KọbiChukwudi** to Kobe, to mention a few.

The Igbos do not wait three days to name a child. And they do not wait seven days before performing the naming ceremony like the Yorubas. When an Igbo child is born, the child is named on the day he or she is born. The name could have been chosen before the child was born. The naming ceremony is called **ikuputa nwa.**

Ikuputa nwa is performed inside the first or second month after the birth of the child. At this gathering, baby powder is sprinkled on the necks or on the desired part of the guests' bodies. The spraying of baby powder signifies the initial presentation of the child to the guests. And everyone sings and dances to upbeat songs.

In the United States and some parts of Europe, this gathering of **ikuputa nwa** among the Igbos is also very festive. The younger generation rarely incorporates the use of baby powder. Some men pass cigars (an inherited English tradition). Dollar bills, Pound Sterlings are also sprayed on the parents and the baby, as a symbol of prosperity for the family through the child.

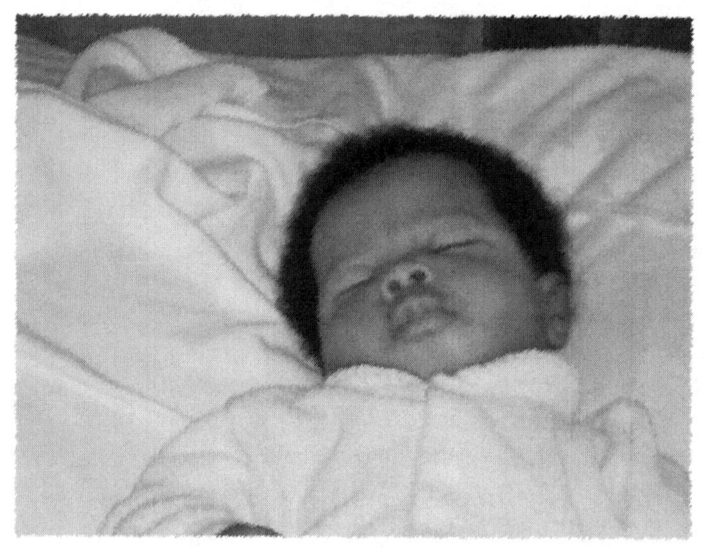

In the photo: A male child named ***KaobiChukwudi***
meaning: ***How God's heart is… nothing compares.***

In the United States of America, people are beginning to appreciate names that appear and sound foreign to them, especially when they are told of the meanings behind the names. Some of them are quick to embrace these names. In some instances, some Americans are known to adopt foreign, great sounding names for their own offsprings. They love all the implied goodness that the names portray and signify.

The traditional ways of naming a child in Igboland are not completely broken. The new generation could be learning something. The stories in the names may differ, but the meanings and the symbols behind them are still the same. A person's name is one's identity. *When choosing a name, choose it rightly.*

CHAPTER 3

TRADITIONAL MARRIAGE IN IGBOLAND

'IGBA-NKWỤ/IME EGO'

This is a must attend ceremony. **Igba-Nkwụ** is simply a magnificent event. Traditional marriage is accepted in the African communities and yes, by God (Genesis 24:53). In the old days, and even in these modern times, when a young man reaches the marrying age, his family advises him (or, he is pressured) to find a wife. Most times, this pressure becomes a quest. And when he chooses the woman he wants as his wife, he takes the next step to inform his family and the elders.

The groom-to-be formally introduces his bride-to-be to his family. He does that in the hope that everyone in his family welcomes her with open arms. In some cases, not everyone embraces the bride-to-be for different reasons. But with nothing to stop the groom from getting hitched, *the die is always cast.* Thereafter, the bride-to-be informs her family about the marriage proposal she had been hit with. The two families decide on a date when the groom-to-be, his immediate family members, and well-wishers, would go to the bride's family **(ndi ọgọ)** and make their intention known. The groom would come bearing gifts; kegs of palmwine, and tons of food, to make a formal proposal, with regards to the beautiful maiden they had seen *three market days ago.*

On this visit, the groom-to-be goes with his father and uncles, to his future in-law's home. In most cases, and depending on each family, no female is allowed to go with the men. Some of the items the groom's family presents to the bride's family must include kola nut. Kola nut signifies life, peace and unity. On the train are; palm wine, and a local vodka-tasting brew, known as **kai-kai.** Other alcoholic beverages are added to complete the list.

It is the job of an elder from the groom's side, to tell the future in-laws that their son has found *a ripened fruit in their garden ready to be plucked.* The bride-to-be is asked to come and say hello to their guests. She will then be asked if she knows the man in question, and if she accepts his hand in marriage. If her answer is yes, the ceremony continues. Finally, the bride's family entertains their in-laws with traditional, mouth-watering appetizers, foods with real bite, and drinks with hooves on.

After the first formal introduction, both families embark on a background check. Both families must be free from any abomination/taboo that could cause potential issues and cause the marriage not to happen. Yes, the background checks determine if a marriage between the families would hold or not. If nothing aborminable is found, the marriage proposal is moved a notch higher; another formal date is set for a second visit.

The second visit is grander, as in a large entourage of guests. Well-wishers are added to the list of attendees. The groom and his family are given a list of items to buy to appease some members of the bride's family. The bride's family gets these as gifts. Should gifts not exchange hands, the festivities could stall...however, momentarily. The gifts range from extra gourds of palm wine (**nkwụ-enu** or **mmanya nkwụ),** cigarettes and **anwụrụ (ground cigarette)** to kola nuts (**ọji**). In some families, the list would include different types of alcoholic and non-alcoholic drinks for the bride's immediate and extended families; for example, **mmanya ụmụnne (maternal wine)** and **ụmụnna (paternal wine**). In some Igbo States, the list might include suitcases of expensive women's fabrics, stockfish, food items etc.

Nevertheless, there are some traditional marriages performed in absentia where the couples to be married live in foreign lands. If that were the case, the **igba nkwụ**; the ceremony itself, doesn't suffer; it carries on as if the bride and groom are physically present.

The bride price/dowry (**ime ego**) is the token that binds a man and a woman in the union of marriage. This paying of the dowry is never ceremonial; it is as much a big part of the marriage rite that must take place to advance things. In the Igbo tradition, the amount to be paid as bride price is always left in the hands of the groom's family. But don't expect to get away by offering what amounts to a pittance to the bride's family.

The dowry depends on the bride's family. Although, the amount paid does not necessarily have to be excessively large. Yet, in today's society, poverty and greed could have increased the amount of the bride price. It makes some brides look like they are being sold to the highest bidders.

However, if the dowry is paid before, or on the day of **igba nkwụ**, she is officially a married woman.

The occasion on this day is a stately affair, and usually grand in scope. There are invited dance groups, and/or solo artists who are paid to perform. A group of friends of the bride are in uniforms called the ***aso-ebi*** group; a borrowed Yoruba term. The bride and groom wear identical traditional outfits. Although, in some instances, they are free to wear any outfit of their choosing. Believe this; this is one day the bride is allowed to flaunt her taste in clothing and accessories. One could tell the bride from a bevy of females in the crowd, just by the way she wears her hair on this day. Initially, the bride is seen wearing an outfit distinguishing her from every female in the crowd as she greets her in-laws. With that taken care of, she would retire to return, fresher, even more gorgeous looking in another outfit, as she makes another grand entrance in search of her husband-to-be.

The Master of Ceremony announces that the bride is about to make a second entrance. Palm wine is poured in a calabash cup by her father or uncle, that is, if her father is deceased. The cup of wine is given to the bride. She is asked to take a sip, and with that, the guests and hosts wouldn't be able to sit still. The moment of truth has truly arrived; didn't they see the groom the last time he was here to announce his intentions? Hadn't they checked his background and that of his entire family? Why would they now stretch their necks looking for him as if he was unknown and had come in, fresh from…? Well the bride is on a mission, and the crowd is all too eager to believe that someone had really come for her hand in marriage. The scene is usually tinged with frozen smiles, and the moment she finally finds him, the crowd starts to breath again. It is funny, but it does happen; and has happened in similar situations, where eligible and not so eligible men in the mix would ask her to bring the wine over to them instead. It is all part of the big fun. Small banter accompanies her search and discovery. When she finds her groom, the crowd rolls into a joyous frenzy; they will shout, clap, and watch with gaping mouths, as the groom accepts the gourd of wine and drinks from it. More spirited ovation follows. The groom will return the empty gourd to the bride's father of course, with enough money he believes the wine he had consumed was worth.

However, it would be an abomination, should the bride drink from the cup of wine, and gave the cup to someone else other than the supposed groom. In the same way, if the groom were to reject the cup of wine offered to him, the marriage dies a sudden death.

After he accepts the cup and drinks from it, the bride sits next to her husband. Live music performers and other forms of entertainment are all in the mix. Food is served in immeasurable quantities. It is usually an eclectic combination of traditional soups and meat, smoked fish, and that brand known as stock fish. Oh my God… bitter leaf soup (**onugbo** soup); **Ọra** soup, **Ọkrọ** (okra) soup, Melon soup (**egusi** soup) and/or **Nsala** soup; a borrowed dish from Calabar, in Cross River State, all served with **fufu**, Tapioca or Grated cassava (**abacha**). Others on the caboose include **Ụgba** and stockfish over **Abacha** with black beans (**akidi**).

You want more? You will get more.

Moi-moi and **jollof** rice aplenty! To top it all off, all local brews are matched with imported wines. The newest couple in town performs their first traditional dance, money is sprayed. Then, one begins to see the first sign that the day would eventually come to an end. Yes, darkness has reared up, and the moment has come for the elders to bless the union before them. If you have patience, this is where you'd need it: The process is protracted because here is where words are spoken, in measured bites. Words assume other terms; they have wings, and are nearly incomprehensible. That is what some listeners would tell you because they wonder with gaping, toothed grins, what the Sage had said. But, for the elders among them, the scene is imbued with words of wisdom, and the words should be spoken tersely, and for certain ears only.

Finally, the new bride bids her family goodbye. At this point, the bride, her family and friends are emotional. When she follows her husband outside to the car, you'd hear cries where some are stifling sobs; tears of joy.

The celebration continues in her new home, on the same evening, to welcome her into her new family. The next day, the new wife is expected to do chores like sweeping the family compound to remind everyone that a new wife has arrived in the family, and that she is marking her territory. Now that the traditional marriage is over, the couple would decide if there would be a church wedding or not. A new life has begun. The wife would assume on a new name; a surname, to reflect that she now belongs to the family she had married into.

CHAPTER 4
IGBO CULTURE IN DIASPORA

Though thousands of miles away, Nigerians in the United States have made America their home away from home. Many Nigerians who live in the States longer than one thousand moons may have lost a tad of their African accent they brought with them from the motherland. True enough, everything is not lost; many Nigerians have found ways to celebrate their customs and tradition, even as they are severely constrained.

Here in the States, especially during summer time, Igbos celebrate festivals like Igbo Day. New Yam Festival (**iri ji ọhụ**) is one of the most celebrated festivals you'd see them celebrating every year. One should not forget the traditional marriage rites (**igba nkwụ**). The marriage rites ceremony is one outing that has all of its original facets still attached to it.

In Houston, Texas, an Igbo social group called **Ndi-Ichie** created IGBO FEST. This festival happens once every year. It is designed to showcase traditional dance groups, like the most popular of them all, the **Atili Ọgwụ**. The bulk of this celebration is aimed at involving children, young adults, in the cultural activities of the Igbo people.

When it comes to masquerades...the Igbos reign supreme. These masquerades like **Adanma**; the beautiful feminine-looking masquerade, moves her body with subtle ease, and dances so effortlessly, you'd believe she was truly a female. And then, you have the **Agaba**. This masquerade is adorned with heavy metal accessories, and more; a machete dangles from its left ear, a double-edged slasher that embellishes other lesser ornamentations with equally evil bearings. Put together, they make this contorted monster's face look like the mangled countenance of an orangutan. *The façade is a true caricature of any imaginable evil, o*nly this time, it is for entertainment. Also, on the menu on this great festive day are gourmet Igbo foods.

Igbo women are known to have huge gatherings. They love it. On such wildly celebrated occasions, they wear mesmerizing and captivating attires to go with the hot-on-the-platter dishes. There are different associations and organisations invited to grace the party on the day of the event. These organizations include: **Ụmụada Igbo Nigeria, Ụmụada Enugu**, **Ụmụada Igbo, Nkwere Daughters, Arọ Women, ArọNdizuọgụ Women, Anambra State Association Women** and many others**.**

Igbo men will not be out-done by these women groups. They have their own associations and social clubs: **Ndi- Ichie Cultural Club**, **People's Club of Nigeria**, **The Lords**, **First Senators of Houson**, **Inc., and The Senators**, to name a few.

Nonetheless, **Ụmụ Igbo Unite** '*provides a community for Cultural Awareness, Networking, Socializing and Intellectual Growth through the care and nurturing of each other as well as through Constructive Discussions, Activities and Showcases. Our membership targets people from all parts of the South-Eastern Igbo speaking states of Nigeria including: Abia, Anambra, Delta, Ebonyi, Enugu, Imo, Bayelsa, Akwa-Ibom,Cross-River and Rivers states. Every year, Ụmụ Igbo Unite hosts an annual convention aimed at promoting unity and networking between young Igbo professionals, and college students.*'

Although thousands of miles away from home, the immigrant-Igbos have done a pretty good job of keeping their home-grown traditions and customs alive. Your root does not determine where you are going. It will simply help keep you grounded, and would ocassionally nudge you not to forget who you really are.

Part Two
A Collection of Inspirational Stories

CHAPTER 5

EVERYDAY MIRACLE

Each day comes with its own gifts. **Ijeamaka**, *aka* **Ije** (**This journey is good/beautiful**) sat next to a Chinese man on the plane on her trip to Atlanta, Georgia. He assisted her in putting her carry-on luggage in the overhead compartment.

'Thank you,' she said, and took her seat. He ignored her. It could be he understood little or no English, Ije thought. Then, she saw an opening and went for it when she said, ***'xiè xie.'*** Her eyes were on him, hoping he had heard her stilted Mandarin.

But the man was as hard as a piñata. He sat nearly stone-faced, gazing at nothing in particular without responding. She decided not to intrude, but never stopped staring at him through blank, naked eyes. After a while, she let a tiny smile escape her. You would think she was gearing up to ask him a question. The urge to engage this man was driving her up the proverbial wall. She had questions framed, and her lips quavered as the words seemed to be looking for a way out. *How do the Chinese name their babies?* She pursed her lips and just as she stared at him once again, she changed her mind. *This man seems cold, and doesn't look too happy.* She could be right. The man had uttered neither word nor a smile.

An hour and a half into the flight, Ije finally figured out a way to make the man open up; she got a sticky note from her purse, wrote something on it and gave it to him. The note read: *'A smile does not cost a thing.'* He looked at her, put the sticky note in his pocket, and still uttered no word.

Ije assumed either his heart was overworked with unimaginable sorrow, or that he was simply unfriendly. She did not know what to do, even as the need to get him to smile swelled in her. She said a little prayer in her heart, and then said,

"I have three children."

She told him how her youngest son would play the role of a drive-thru Burger King customer with his siblings, and then would ask his older sister to be one of the employees.

Big sister: 'Welcome to Burger King, may I take your order?'

Son: 'I want #3, no pickle, no onion, just ketchup and mayo please, and sprite too. Thank you.'

Ije's face lit up, eyes trained on the stranger without a smile. Her hope riding a crest, knowing she had probably said the right things to burst him wide open with a come-from-the-heart story of his life.

At some point, she stopped to gauge him, and then saw to her amazement, a smile wider than his face could carry. Yes, the stone-faced man had warmed up and could be finally ready to tell the story of his life.

Thank you Father. That was a quick one! She mumbled, knowing her God heard her.

"That is one funny little boy. Smart too."

Ije beamed, stuck her hand out and introduced herself.

"Hello, my name is Ije."

"I am Chui." He muttered. "Your son… how old is he?"

"He is 5 going on fifteen."

Mr. Chui smiled at that, then pushed his head backward and shut his eyes. He could have moved into one of his quiet moments again. Ije chose not to bother him. She pulled out her Ipod, stuck the ear-piece into her ears and fell backward herself, matching Mr. Chui's benign repose.

A few minutes into her short nap, she heard repeated sniffs. It sounded like someone was crying. She thought it was all in her short reverie. But, it turned out the sniffs were coming from the man sitting next to her. It was Mr. Chui. Her heart quietly broke for him.

"What's the matter?" She asked him. Clearly, the man was in some kind of hurt.

"I am jealous of you," he began. "I have no family to go home to," he concluded.

Ije shut her eyes after she heard Mr. Chui.

"I had a family once."

"You did?"

"Yes, a wife and two sons."

Ije believed that something terrible had to have happened to Mr. Chui's family. Her hand went to her mouth to stifle the gasp looking to escape her.

She was quick to prayer; this one was a long entreaty, and she was hoping that God didn't have much on His Hands at that very moment. Ije had struck gold: Mr. Chui opened up to her, holding nothing back. His heart was indeed deeply burdened.

MR. CHUI'S TALE

A couple of years ago, Mr. Chui migrated to the United States with his family of four; his wife and two sons. Shortly after the family's migration, he took them back to China, on a summer vacation. Mr. Chui and his entire family had walked into a hornet's nest, literally speaking.

On a short taxi ride to Huaxi, his village, the worst had happened. The taxi his family was riding in drove straight into a vicious gun battle between two rival gangs. They were caught in the middle of a turf war with nowhere to run to. When the firing ceased, and the smoke had cleared, the body count included everyone in the taxi, except for Mr. Chui's. He had survived the onslaught with just the scrapes he sustained from glass falling on him. His whole family was wiped out.

Ije was crying softly.

Mr. Chui expressed how happy he was when he realized his wife was pregnant with the twins. He chose names for the twins; names that would depict the kind of men they could be in the future.

"I was finally a papa," he had said, with tears filling his eyes. "After years of loving and caring for my family, I had to lose them the way I did. A few seconds was all it took."

He wondered why his life was spared on that faithful day. "Now, I exist as a shell of who I used to be as a human being."

Ije held his hand and asked him to please look at her. He did. Ije moaned her plea.

"I am truly sorry for your loss. I cannot imagine how you must be feeling, but I understand that you have a big hole in your heart. You must find something else to fill it." Ije pleaded, and continued. "Life is hope. Find a way to be a part of life again. You must do more than just exist, Mr. Chui." She squeezed his hand in hers, and then began to massage it, deliberately. "I will remember you, especially in my prayers," she said through clenched teeth, and then let his hand go.

Mr. Chui smiled. She had gotten to him. Her own face lit up; overwhelmed by a host of passion that was forcing their way into her. Ije spoke, only this time, Mr. Chui could have wondered if she had spoken in Latin.

"**Chi nọnyelụ gi**," she intoned.

"Huh?" He said.

She apologized, but didn't lose a bit. Mr. Chui wanted to know what the words meant.

"God be with you," she said.

"If we had time on our hands, I'd prefer…"

Ije cut him off, but dropped a smile to humor him. "Would you rather I teach you a few words in my language?"

But, Mr. Chui had a different idea instead. He would rather listen to what she was listening to on her Ipod.

"Your music, what's your taste in music? I am just curious."

"I don't want you going through a cultural shock, Mr. Chui."

"Do not be surprised if I told you I have a collection of the Funkmeister's CDs."

"Rick James?"

"No, the Godfather himself…"

"Oh… James Brown?"

"Yeah, only I would have wanted him to do a piece, you know; *I'm Chinese and proud*."

"You are funny, Mr. Chui. Here, you can listen now. Just hoping you don't get disappointed."

Ije watched him with rapt attention, as Mr. Chui's head bopped and swayed to the rhythm of the beat he was listening to. And he had a smile to go with his joy.

For Ije, she was relieved, and glad the man who had known so much pain could find time to *shoo* in a different kind of emotion from the one he had been living with. They were running out of time. With just five minutes to the end of the flight, Ije took a moment to explain to Mr. Chui the meaning of some of the songs he had been listening to, especially that piece of grooving lyrics by a young, aspiring Nigerian artist, Obiora Obiwon.

Parts of the lyrics Ije translated were Igbo phrases and words Mr. Chui wanted translated. Phrases like; "**Obi mụ o**: **My Heart**. **Nkechinyere mụ o**: **The one that God has given me. Ọmalicha**: **Beautiful one**. **Nwanyi Ọma**: **Good woman**. **Nwoke Ọma**: **Good man**. **Ezigbo enyi mụ**: **My good friend**. **Ụsọ mụ**: **My love**. **Ọnye nke nhụrụ na-anya**: **The one that I love**.

"Oh my Gosh, I love this song." Ije muttered.

"Me too," Mr. Chui said, and then he grabbed the ear piece. He wasted no time, sticking it into his ears. The song he was listening to could have caused him to sit up, if he didn't have ants in his pants. He stared blankly at Ije with a face only his mother would love, mouthing soundlessly while pointing a crooked finger to his right ear piece.

"I love you…" Mr. Chui intoned. His finger still aimed at his ear.

Ije dropped back, shifted her gaze from him for a second, and then turned, however gracefully to look him in the eye.

"What…?" Ije asked, hoping the affable Mr. Chui hadn't lost his mind.

He yanked the piece from his ear, smiling broadly.

"Wow!" he exclaimed. "The song is fresh, dew-on-green-grass fresh," Mr. Chui said.

"Which of the songs is that?"

"The one about 'I love you…"

Ije exhaled deeply. Her face was no longer weary, just profound with open delight.

"Glad you like it, Mr. Chui."

Finally Mr. Chui said, this time with a wider smile on his face, "Miss Ije, **xiè xiè**."

On their way out of the airplane, she gave him for his listening pleasure; two music CDs that were both done in Igbo. She also handed him something extra; a music video. She was certain the video would entertain him, especially since a great part of the song and dance had to be new to him, even with his experiences listening to the Godfather of soul.

"I hope we would have a second opportunity to sit together again… in a longer flight," he said.

"Fate… fate… don't underestimate fate, Mr. Chui. I could be the Angel of God sent here to warm you up, you know… to heal you from all that pain," Ije said, patting him on his shoulder.

The erstwhile steely Mr. Chui had to stop tears from running loose.

"God…?" He asked, not sure if he could repeat the name. But he did. "Did you say God, Ms. Ije?"

"Yes. God! I'm sure He had a Hand in us meeting today."

"I don't believe…" He stopped himself.

"You don't believe what? In God…?"

"Yes." He said looking away from her, afraid he had annoyed her. But, he was quick to add:

"…but not anymore. Not anymore, Ms. Ije. I have not laughed nor smiled in a long time; at least since my family died so violently. But today, maybe, your God smiled on me, and I am inclined to believe that He is."

CHAPTER 6
A STORY BEHIND A NAME

In Africa, there are stories behind the naming of a child. Most times, circumstances are used to determine the name given to the newborn.

One summer time, **Nkemakọlam**, *aka* **Nkem**,

(May I never lack what belongs to me) visited Nigeria after having lived in the States for several years. Two nights after she arrived in her village, she met an extra-ordinary woman. She was eighty-nine years old. Her trip would change dramatically thereafter. The old woman had a story to tell.

She was a great grand-mother. She had recognized Nkem because she looked like someone she knew from long time ago. She was talking about Nkem's great-grand mother. She gave Nkem a preview of her life story.

Her name was Edna Ugonma (**Ugonma** means: **Beauty; like an eagle**). Ugonma was 17 when she met her 42 year old husband who already had six wives. She became the 7th wife to this farmer. For six years, she was unable to carry pregnancies to term. She consistently miscarried. At the time, modern medicine was not advanced. There was no way of determining what was causing the miscarriages. Only decades later, was it known, with certainty, that she could have had an Incompetent cervix. In case, the procedure; Cerclage could have been used to protect her cervix and her babies. Incompetent cervix is when the cervix dilates, usually at twenty weeks into the pregnancy. Cerclage, an encircling wire loop or ring, is used to prevent the cervix from opening up. This way, the fetus is protected, and the pregnancy would have a better chance at reaching full term. However, there are no guarantees. The chances are simply better.

After Ugonma lost her sixth child, the grapevine came alive with despicable rumors. The other wives saw an opening and exploited it. They literally told their husband that Ugonma was a witch, and was *eating* all her unborn children through witchcraft. Bear in mind that during this time, Christianity had not taken root, especially in Ugonma's neck of the woods. People at that time worshipped hand-crafted dieties that sat fixated under trees. Some are molded out of clay, and placed in a corner of the compound. Everyday, the clay head is fed blood from sacrificial chickens and goats. It was in one of these shrines that her husband took her to swear before the oracle that she had nothing to do with the calamity that had befallen her.

Ugonma cried and pleaded with her husband and his kinsmen not to make her swear before an oracle everyone believed would snap your head in your sleep, if you had as much as slipped into a small lie to embellish your oath. She cried and lifted her voice; asking neighbouring dieties to come to her aid. Finally, she was dragged to the shrine. The chief priest, a bony, frail piece of humanity, scared Ugonma even more. She was forced to prostrate before the shrine and swear to the god that she had nothing to do with any of her pregnancy mishaps. While she swore, she did so in the name of honesty, and intergrity. She called the god of thunder; **AMADIỌHA**, to hear her plea. In the chaos, no one knew that Ugonma was pregnant; not even Ugonma knew of her situation.

Few weeks later, her pregnancy became obvious. Naturally, everyone but Ugonma assumed that it was the oracle that had rewarded her; it was the oracle's way of telling her husband and the rest of the village elders that Ugonma had nothing to do with the miscarriages she had suffered.

"Now I know differently," Ugonma said, staring into Nkem's eyes.

"What do you know different?" Nkem asked.

"That there was a different God who saved me from the snares of the devil during those trying times. He was there with me when all hope was lost. When we least expect a miracle to happen, God shows up. He would rewrite the quotients in a bad drama to set the record straight. He clearly did that in my case. With me, He left His mark. We must remember that God is never late. We need to learn to persevere and remain faithful. Most times, He alters our path to get us to the right destination. Naturally, as human beings, we are so very impatient. We try different things to achieve a goal. But when the right time comes, God removes the blockades and allows us to get to our destinations just like He intended," Ugonma had said.

Patience is indeed a virtue, and perseverance is hard work. Ugonma persevered, and in the end, she was blessed with twin boys. "God proved to the world that I was not a witch, and despite my imperfections, God blessed me with children and grandchildren," she said. She named the twins; **ỌnyedikaChukwu (Who is like God**?) and **Zikọra** (Full name:

Zikọra/na/ibụ/Chim: Show the world that you are my God). In the end, she had five children. Each child was given a name that glorified God, and told the story of Ugonma's life.

Naturally, the villagers who were idol worshippers at the time assumed that their oracle had blessed Ugonma with the twins, and had given her more children.

"The one who argues with a fool is no different from the fool." Ugonma said and fell silent. She knew in her heart that God was faithful and had blessed her with the fruits of her womb.

Nkem was amazed at Ugonma's life experiences, especially how she had weathered the storm that was set to consume her. Nkem understood that there is a reason for every season. She had no doubt that God had rescued Ugonma, even when her people didn't know Him. God didn't abandon her, even when all she knew about any diety was relegated to simple acts of pouring libation to wooden gods on her husband's front yard.

"Thank You Jesus." Nkem said, and gave her a bear hug. "It is an honor to have met a woman like you."

Ugonma had lived a very painful life as a young adult and as one of the wives of a farmer. She went through life's hurdles with weighty, psychological impairments. She was in the middle of every storm that passed and each left her with a broken heart. She never experienced the true joy of being a wife without the suspicion of being a witch in her own home. She had no choice, but to remain in an unhealthy marriage for one simple reason: She had nowhere else to go.

"Where else could I have gone?" she had asked. "Many women who stay in unhealthy marriages do so for all the wrong reasons," Ugonma had said.

It's been five years since Ugonma told her story to Nkem. A lot did change in her life. Of course, she had grown older and with all her faculties intact. The fruits of her endurance are there for us to see. They took care of her. With time, the same children she had reared had moved on; all grown up and immeasurably successful in their various endeavours.

In the end, Ugonma died a happy woman, having lived to the ripeful age of ninety-four years.

CHAPTER 7
THE THIN LINE

"The tongue has the power of life and death and those who love it will eat its fruit." Proverbs 18:21. Sometimes, the names we give our children tend to predict their character, and the words that leave our tongues tend to manifest themselves.

It has been proven that the names we give our children at birth could determine how they live their lives. There is nothing scientific about this claim. The Igbos also believe strongly that words out of a person's mouth, even the name given to a child has ways of living out its meaning. For instance, when a child is named **Sọnma (Simply beautiful)**, her behavior is expected to match the kind of beauty that signifies the true meaning of the name she was given. Sọnma signifies a female child who is as beautiful as beyond words can describe, and/or, that she possesses the sweetest of dispositions and countenances that are unmatched.

On the same note, another child is named Sọnma after her mother, as a way of honoring the woman who bore her. The irony of this is that the female child is so named in hope that she would grow up and resemble her mother's beauty and geniality. All hopes could be dashed, when the child grows up, and looks or behaves nothing like her mother. The child's measurable attributes and endowments could all have come from somewhere outside her mother's genetic pool. The meaning and purpose of her given name; Sonma, is therefore defeated.

On August 15, 2010, "One of world's leading poets of Nigerian descent Prof. **Chukwudubem** *aka* **Dubem Agha Okafọr**, 64, shot his wife, Cheryl V. Okafor, 37, then turned the gun on himself after a heated argument at his relative's house in Reading, Pennsylvania," Investigators said. Chukwudubem means **God, lead/guide me**. **Agha**, his middle name which means **war**, could have been the negative force that led him into committing such mindless violence. No one is sure if it was truly the case with the professor, but the probability remains haunting.

Another instance of the impact of a name would be the name usually given to baby girls; **Ọbiageli (One born into wealth/prosperity)**. This name can also be understood to mean; **a guest will eat** (as in when he/she visits your home. In the Igbo language, **Ọbia** means **a guest**. Therefore, a guest must be entertained with food and wine. **...geli** always stood for; **will eat**.

In this story, **Nwakaego** *aka* **Ego (A child is greater/more valuable than money)**, was born into a middle-class family. Her appetite for the finer things in life was legendary. Nwakaego had insatiable desires. She chose the wrong path to achieve her goals, and completely fell off the tracks. Nwakaego forgot her morals and was ethically deficient in all her dealings, as she sought for ways to increase her fold. She was never satisfied with whatever she had, and was consistently looking for ways to strike it richer. The woman was without shame. She wanted to acquire more, and it drove her her to places only a filthy mind would dare. As a consequence, she became a call girl. When that didn't go far enough, and when she had saved enough money to run a brothel, she bought one. Nwakaego became a madame, running the notorious hangout for men, a Cathouse known as De Lounge Suites, in Victoria Island, Lagos.

Basically, the true meaning of her name was a diametric opposite to the way she chose to live her life. She had the perfect name for the imperfect behavior. She was tagged '**Ọbiageli**.'

CHAPTER 8

WANNABES

It was an exciting new adventure for young **IkeChi (The strength of God)**. He had just turned nine years old, and was on his way with his parents to Disney World. His birthday would be celebrated there.

IkeChi grew up in a home where English was the first language and his native tongue was not even offered to him as an option. His parents spoke in Igbo to each other, but communicated to their children in English. This language was therefore, the main language spoken in their home. This nine-year old boy could not speak nor write anything in the Igbo language.

Disney World… awesome! Just like young IkeChi had imagined it. It was everything he saw on television and more. Incidentally, he ran into a few Nigerian children of the Igbo descent. They played together and conversed plentifully. All conversations were in English.

Two days into their trip, IkeChi had an encounter that would stay with him for the rest of his life. He would learn from this. He went into one of the rides with children his age. It was one of those scary rides, but nevertheless an exciting one. When the ride was over, it was time for the young generation to mingle and make new friends.

The temperature was hot and humid. Despite that, everyone was having a great time, except IkeChi. He was quiet all of a sudden and did not want to play with his friends or get on any more rides. He just felt like going back home to Nigeria where he believed he would be most comfortable. His parents could not figure out what had happened on the playground to have caused their son to turn moody all of a sudden. It was in IkeChi's nature to be happy and playful at all times. His parents were clearly bothered by his sudden indifference, and nudged him to explain his sudden mood change. He had nothing to say. All he wanted was to leave the relative safety of all that had been provided for him by his parents and go back to a country he barely knew. The next day, he refused to leave his hotel room, sobbing for hours on end.

On the second day, IkeChi's lips parted. He was talking and talking, as would a screaming banshee. "Mom, why did you not teach me my language?" he asked, daring his mother to come with an excuse. "You talk to dad and all your friends in Igbo!"

Of course, mom was speechless, clearly hesitant to respond. She felt embarrassed, aware that she had failed her son. However, when she spoke, she did so, condescendingly, as a way of exculpating herself from her failures. That didn't help much. She dropped the act.

"IkeChi, I realize now that your father and I had made a mistake. We should have taught you the Igbo language. I thought speaking the English language would be of benefit to you more than the language of your ancestors. We were wrong."

IkeChi cried out, miming;

"You know what this has done to me, mom?"

"I am not sure that I do, son."

"My friends were making fun of me for not being able to speak my native language.' I am caught between two worlds, and neither am I proficient in both. Mom, maybe you've not heard it, I have an Igbo accent, yet I cannot speak Igbo. And with the English language, I still have a long way to go. A lot of times, they didn't understand me when I spoke. I was embarrassed."

Mom and dad were the ones more embarrassed, even heartbroken to an extent. One good thing from this exchange was that IkeChi's parents made a decision to start communicating with their son in the Igbo language. IkeChi was enrolled in a summer program to help him learn the Igbo language.

Is it now late for IkeChi to learn? No, it is never too late to learn, *unless of course, one has used six parts of one's life*. It has been proven that it is easier teaching a child a new language in early childhood. You should wonder why most parents of the Igbo descent do not abide by this tenet. IkeChi could have been dealt an irreversible blow, and might not be able to learn the Igbo language, no matter how diligent he took his new role. But, he had gone into the program a determined young boy. His success will depend on how much support, as in home tutoring, his parents give him.

This should serve as a lesson for every parent, African, and non-African, who chooses to replace their native tongue with a language that is not theirs. To incorporate a foreign language into a household is a good thing. But, when parents embrace it to assuage an inferiority complex to fit in, and totally ignore their native tongue, there is a price to be paid. The consequences of alienation in this regard are immeasurable. As we have seen with IkeChi's situation, they can be devastating. Parents need to assume the responsibility to be good teachers and role models for their children. If nothing is done to break the fetters of this neo-enslavement, most tribal languages could be lost.

CHAPTER 9
WHEN HARRY MET AKU

Harry is an African-American male married to a Nigerian-American woman of the Igbo extraction. Her name is **Chinelo**, literally meaning: **God decides or the Will of God**. She is known by her English name, Linda. Linda was born and raised in America, and like most, does not know how to speak the Igbo language, her mother-tongue. Her parents did not expose her to the Igbo language at an early age, and neither was she taught the language as a young adult. She would pick up bits and pieces of it during her yearly visits to Nigeria with her husband.

During one of such visits, Harry met an Igbo girl, who at the time was as old as his wife, Linda. They struck a friendship. Her name is **AkụChukwu**, *aka* **Akụ**, **(God's wealth)**. Not long after that, Harry would find time, and would send for Aku. She came, and in some instances, would have lunch or supper with him and his family. They had become close buddies, and would talk for hours on end, sorting the differences in African and American cultures. Aku gave Harry an Igbo name, more like a name to endear him with. It stuck. Akụ called Harry, **Chukwueloka** *aka* **Eloka**, meaning: **The depth of God's council**.

Harry was very excited and requested that it all be written down for easy access. He would like to surprise his wife someday with the Igbo phrases he had learned.

Not long after she had set Harry on his way to learning these words and phrases, Harry was showing an imposing dexterity in his pronounciations of this once esoteric lingo. Akụ was impressed, and Harry was so excited. His wife, Linda, must hear him. But, he must wait until they arrived back in the States. He would pick the time and place to *blow her mind* with his newly acquired prowess.

Six weeks later, Harry and Linda returned back to the States. Harry recused himself from the situations that would prematurely give his secret away. His Igbo word power was increasing in leaps, and he had begun to mouth them as he did one thing or the other, even talking to himself, as in soliloquy. *Yes, when the day comes, Harry will be ready.*

January 2000, right after the New Year's celebration, Harry decided to take Linda to the Lakeshore, in Oakland, California. The waterfront was densely populated on this day. He grabbed her hand, pulled her close and whispered into her ear:

"**Ezigbo m… Ọmalicham… Nwanyi ọma… Ọnye nke nhụrụ n'anya**," he began.

But Linda pulled away from him like she had been stung by a bee. Her jaw dropped; her hands flailing, waiting for the words, any word to rescue her from her totally catatonic state. Moments later, she recovered. Linda grabbed his hand, pulled him against her, kissing him full in the mouth. After the smooching, she had the words that would liberate her;

"Where and when did you learn to speak my language, Harry?"

"Akụ was my teacher."

"And she thought you words like; **My Love… My beautiful one… Beautiful woman… The one that I love**? Wow!" Then, she kissed him again.

"So, how did I do?"

"**Ezigbo m, i melụ ọfụma**. You did great, my love."

"**Daalụ**," Harry was quick to say.

Harry and Linda's love grew. She became more interested in learning her native language. They tried to always communicate in the Igbo language, as a way of bonding even more. He learned a lot from his wife too, and soon enough, the English language barely saw the light of day in their home. It looked as if they had found what was missing in their marriage and relationship.

And yes, your guess is as good as the Writer's… Linda took in, and nine months later, she had a baby girl; **Sọnirụ** meaning **Forward ever, backward never**."

CHAPTER 10

CHINELO: THE WILL OF GOD

Just like our faces and names are different, so are our stories and destinies. We all do have a story, or stories to tell. **Ifeọma (Something good)** was a very pleasant woman with a positive take on life. She was married to **Obinna (Father's heart)** for many years, eighteen to be exact. She was unable to conceive a child due to reasons not genetically attributed to her. The reason: Obinna had a low sperm count and was unable to impregnate his wife. His parents were unaware of their son's predicament and was as always, blaming the usual suspect; the woman.

In most West African nations, it is always assumed that it is the woman's fault if she was childless, regardless of the reason behind her infertility. And, when she does have children, and they happen to be all females, the blame game continues; she is incapable of having a male child. It was so with Ifeoma. She was blamed for not giving their son, Obinna, a child. For years, she lived with and endured the snide remarks that came with it. The condemnation never waned; it raised its head with every new day. Her crime was that she was childless. But, Obinna stood by her and loved her all the same.

Eventually, Ifeọma and Obinna decided that they would take steps to do what the doctors had told them to do: New medication to increase his sperm count, and if Ifeoma didn't conceive, an effective intervention would follow; an Invitro Fertilization (IVF).

They went through many failed insemination attempts. Eventually, their prayer was answered. It took some time, but it happened for them.

Her in-laws' behavior towards Ifeoma flipped; they saw her in a different light. They decided they would accept her, love her as their daughter-in-law because she was finally pregnant, and would soon bear a child.

Ifeoma was aware of her in-laws' hypocritical leanings. She chose to ignore them, and rather focused on the new blessing that God had bestowed upon her.

The birth of their son was not the beginning, but a continuation of God's love in their lives. When God does something in our lives, it is not the beginning of His grace, but a continuation of His gifts to us. His gift of life to each of us is the beginning of His love.

As the author has pointed out in an earlier story, the path to naming a child almost always has a story behind it. The process is nearly sacred, and in some instances, it takes a whole week to prepare and then conduct the ceremony. With Ifeoma's experience, she and her husband chose a meaningful name. They picked one that propagated the virtues of patience and faith. They named their baby boy, **ObiOlisa (God's heart)**.

CHAPTER 11

IJE: THE JOURNEY

MmaOlisa was a woman scorned. It was so for her because of the sins of her fathers'. She was tagged an **'Osu,'** because, the family she was born into was one. In the early days and even today, this social dehumanization and classification of people is still in existence. In Igboland, the practice of sub-humanizing others; the process by which one's humanity is stripped, and then tossed away, as if given to the desert vultures to consume, is still prevalent.

In Nigeria, especially among the Igbos, the word "**Osu or Ohu**" means an **outcast** or a **slave**. One way of becoming one is by committing an act that is deemed aborminable. The person is cast away from the village by way of sacrifice to a particular deity. The other sure fire way is to marry into an Osu family. Once one is deemed the property of any diety, this badge of dishonor would remain so. It would, at no time, in the movement of history, change its intended branding. The person sacrificed would no longer belong freely, of course, to the society he/she hailed from. Thereafter, they would live alone because of their implied staled and viled nature. No free minded person in the village would have any use for them. They would have no social life with the rest of the people. Unfortunately, almost every generation of Igbos have upheld this tradition, and would not let the practice die off with time. *God did not create anyone to be 'Cast Away.'*

An Osu is seen as an inoperable cancer. When a person is tagged an Osu, the stain is considered long-lasting, and could never be washed away. From generation to generation, that particular family and the fruits it bears will be seen in the same light. It is similar to a genetic trait that cannot be erased. People would treat the branded family like pariahs. The so-called free families are careful not to have any kind of relationship with anyone who is an Osu.

The word is obscene and inhumane. Many dislike it with passion, but are unable to do anything to stop the carnage it had become. If one is an Osu, you would want to ask yourselves: Who made him/her an Osu? Sadly enough, the same people that treat them heartlessly are the same ones who had fashioned them what they had become.

MmaOlisa (The beauty of God) *aka* **Mma,** lived through her young adult life plagued by this unfortunate branding of her fore-fathers. The love of God was never far from her. She was also an orphan, and had lived on the streets in order to survive. One fateful evening, she was attacked and then raped by three strange men. She believed she knew one of the rapists.

Twelve weeks later, she found out she was pregnant. Her life was over, Mma believed. For the next twenty-eight weeks, she did not receive any kind of pre-natal care. *However, she had someone watching over her.*

Mma went into labor while asleep in the forest. She had cleared a corner in the vast tropical, and was using the spot as shelter. She cried bitterly, not because of the labor pains. She was crying out for help. All Mma could mutter through her endless tears was "**Chim o, ebe ka i nọ**?" (**Oh my God, where are you**?)

Moments later, her prayer was answered. A man cutting woods nearby heard her cries and approached the general area. He found Mma lying helplessly on the forest ground, underneath a makeshift tent. It was still ninety-something degrees under the shade. One look at her, and the man knew she needed help. Nothing was said between them. The man knew what had to be done. The baby had crowned, and the man, although nearly helpless, took a position that would have described him as an arm-chair physician. His hands were in place; spread out underneath her. His mouth was wide open, eyes popped wider than a demitasse spoon. He would lick his lips; bite down on the same lips when he felt fear. Good for him, nature was calling the shots, and he could be following the dictates of that unhearable voice, telling him what to do.

When the baby dropped into his open hands, he held on tight, yet gently, as he stayed with the ebb and flow of a mind that was screaming at him not to drop the newborn.

"**Kedụ ife m mụlụ**…?" Mma asked, through cracked voice. Her head was rising in an effort to see beyond the man's rather large frame.

"It's a boy," he said rather hurriedly, to stop her from asking any more questions.

The man raised his hands, putting the newborn up for Mma to see. Blood was dripping, and a tremendous joy was riding up in the air with it.

He showed Mma her son. She stuck her hands out to receive him, and then pulled back as the man reached into his side pocket for a knife. With the rusted knife, he severed the umbilical cord.

"Why is he not crying?" She asked, losing some of that vaulted spirit.

"Oh, **chelụ**…"

The man slapped the baby's back, hard enough to cause him to cry. Seconds later, the newborn began to cry. Mma stuck her hands out a second time, and he gently placed the fragile humanhood in her hands. With his under shirt, he cleaned the baby up, while he was still in her mother's hands. The man stood up, gauging mother and child with a warm gaze.

"My time with you is up," he had told her, and left the scene. She used her clothes to protect her newborn. She chose the right name. She called him, **Zikọra;** full name: **Zikọra/na/ibụ/Chim (Show the world that you are my God).** *It is indeed amazing how God works His mysteries. He is always on time.*

Zikọra was feeding on his mother's milk, while Mma was rapidly dehydrating. Two days later, Mma and Zikọra were found by a passerby; a Good Samaritan. They were taken to the hospital. The woman who found them took them home with her after their hospital stay. She wasted no time making Mma and her son a part of her family.

This Good Samaritan was God-sent to Mma and her son, as was the man who had originally helped her during Zikora's birth. God showed the world that He is God indeed.

Mma's destination was delayed for a period of time. The devil was in some of these details and would not relent in his competition with God for our souls. There is no questioning the fact that prayer and faith can work wonders. No matter the mark we put on each other, especially the negative ones, God has the ultimate say, and it is His Will that must be done.

Chapter 12

Life: A Gracious Gift

"Ọnweghi ihe bụ ihe ọhụrụ na-okpuru anyanwụ! Ọnweghi ihe anya hụrụ were gbaa mmee: "There's nothing new under the sun. There's nothing that the eye sees, that causes it to bleed." These are some of the famous sayings in Igboland.

A woman named Jessica went into labor at seven and half months. She was a Caucasian-American in Nigeria, on a work-related assignment. She panicked as soon as her water broke, because she had heard horrible stories about the ineffective healthcare services in many parts of Africa.

She was taken to the nearest clinic in the remote village where she was stationed. There was no physician on call that night. Her contractions were coming every one and half minutes. There was a certified nursing assistant (CNA), and a mid-wife on duty, to assist Jessica. The electricity in the area had been out for days, and would not be expected back anytime soon. At the time, the clinic was functioning on a stand-by generator that could barely support the entire facility.

Jessica was completely overwhelmed by intense pain. She was afraid for her unborn baby. The mid-wife assured her that she would do her best to make sure everything went fine. "God is with you on this," the mid-wife said to Jessica to calm her down.

But Jessica was not a believer, and would prefer His name be dropped at the moment. She focused on her pains and fears instead of focusing on God. She screamed until she had no strength in her to scream any longer. The mid-wife was able to calm her to an extent when she began singing an Igbo gospel song, calling on the God Jessica didn't believe in to intercede on her behalf anyway.

"She knows not what she is saying, Father," the Mid-wife sang.

Jessica did not understand one word of the song. But, the melody had ameliorated her pain somehow. Could it be the song was the panacea for her pain? The mid-wife never did let up; she sang with new-found fevor, orchestrating with both hands, as she directed an imaginary, bedside symphony to sing along with her. The room filled up, and Jessica heard other instruments as accompaniments. She was been aided and the once crafty notes that were difficult to hit, flowed through her effortlessly. Jessica was enthralled, and had dissolved into tears, even before she grasped the meaning of the song.

The song went like this:

O Chineke, Chi mara obim o, idiri mụ nma, idighi agbanwe (repeat)

My God, the God that knows my heart, you are good to me, you never change

A chụba gi, a chụba gi, gba ba, gbakwuru Jesus, Onye n'eme nma.

When you are being pursued (*under an attack*), run, run to Jesus. He is kind.

Gbakwuru ya mgbe ichọrọ ya, ọ diri gi mma, ọdighi agbanwe

Run to Him when you need Him. He is good to you. He never changes

Daa n'ụkwụ ya, gwa ya ihe i na-achọ, ọ ga-eme ya, ọdighi agbanwe

Fall at His feet, tell Him your desires, and He will do it. He never changes.

O Chineke, Chi mara obim o, idiri mụ nma o, idighi agbanwe (repeat)

My God, the God that knows my heart, you are good to me, you never change.

Jessica had fallen in love with both the song and the singer. Her pain had not truly vanished; it was only the weight of it that had lessened to a manageable level. With the melody still fresh like the morning dew in her mind, she hummed it, and tried to fashion it into something she could own.

In the end, her baby was delivered, with no complications. She heard the cry of her newborn, and could have believed that the God of the mid-wife could have had a hand in this experience.

Jessica was deeply inspired by what she believed was a near-death experience for her. And for that, she wanted to learn more about the Igbo culture, and the God she didn't believe in. She chose an Igbo name for her daughter; a name that would at no time, call to question, the power of God. She named her **Chiagọziem (God has blessed me)** *aka* **Chi**.

Know this: *God's name is a name above all other names*

CHAPTER 13

DEATH IS NOT THE END...

At every point in time, a life ends, and then another begins. It is the cycle of life. Death is inevitable and must come when it will come. Neither life nor death would exist without the other.

Jared and Hillary were high school sweethearts. They got married right after graduation from college. They both got their dream jobs before moving into their new apartment on West Chester Drive. Money wasn't plentiful, but they were content. The love they had for each other was enough to sustain them.

Hillary got pregnant after they had been married for two years. They were excited. Hillary showed off her pregnancy at work, to anyone with enough time to listen to her. She had the body, so she wore sexy maternity clothing. Maybe, that was why she was keen on showing her protruding stomach. You see, pregnancy looked so beautiful on Hillary, and and she carried it well. At every turn, she looked grander, even gorgeous to her own amazement. Jared loved it too. And he could not have seen his wife look so alluring in all the months of her pregnancy. In the ensuing months, it was safe to assume that parents-to-be were looking forward to the day the new baby would arrive.

At one time during Hillary's pregnancy, they decided they had to know the sex of the baby. It would help them pick a name. But they never did find that out. To them, either sex would be okay. They were happy and looked forward to the day the baby would come.

At thirty-nine weeks, the baby arrived. Hilary and Jared's lives changed. It was a short labor for her; almost an effortless delivery. She had a baby girl. Hillary was exceptionally exhausted, but the sight of her baby laying next to her sustained her. The newborn gave her strength beyond words could describe. They named their baby girl, Jacques.

The Jacques-Cartier River is in the southern part of Quebec, Canada. This was where Hillary and Jared met. Their experience in that one-horse town would live forever in their memories. So, as a way of keeping the flame burning in their minds and hearts, they had no problem naming their little girl after the river.

However, everything that could go wrong went wrong. The erstwhile happy family had their joy and gladness snatched away. Moments after the baby was taken away to be cleaned, and the joyous father had had one cigar after another, Hillary drifted into the throes of a mild shiver. It didn't look like something was seriously wrong with her, not until she started to sweat and convulse did Jared panic. Within minutes, her situation had worsened; her teeth were clenched tight, and the whites of her eyes had become prominent. Jared's eyes were wide open as he sat motionless watching Hillary lose all consciousness. Seconds later, she was dead; an apparent victim of internal bleeding. The doctors had no chance to save her.

Life's unfair! Well, not in all situations, it is not.

Jared was in shock for hours. He had to be sedated. When he finally woke up, his mind was still flying on half-mast. He was unable to discern what had truly happened to him, to cause him to see things in strange combinations. The nightmare was propagated further when his occluded mind would not dissipate with time. As is the case with these kinds of situations, Jared eventually snapped out of it. When he realized he had lost his beloved wife, he cried even more. He asked to see Hillary's dead body one more time. His wish was granted.

Should he blame God? Absolutely not! Everything happens for a reason. Most times, we do not realize it, until the time is right.

On this fateful day, the attending nurse was a Nigerian (Igbo) lady. Her heart went out to Jared as she watched him with his baby. Jared couldn't stop crying, and the nurse could do nothing to comfort him. Those times when the nurse took care of the newborn, she would rock her gently, and mumble inane drivels only she could understand. Actually, she was calling the newborn names; names like **Chizitelụ**. Jared assumed the nurse had drifted into a trance, and the incoherent gibberish coming from her was vintage Hopi Indian, or something straight out of a voodoo song and dance, the way most notorious African Shamans practice their trades. He was done with her irritating incantations, and rushed to retrieve his newborn from her. The nurse understood his feelings. She handed the baby over, and tried to explain to him that the incomprehensible waffle was for the baby, a form of prayer. She was calling his baby the name that graced her tongue, and in a prayerful way. She explained it thus; **Chizitelụ** means **God sent**.

"I know you just lost your wife. Remember, this baby is a gift to you from God. Sometimes in life, we lose something precious to gain something equally precious," she said.

Jared could not help himself. He wept some more, before giving the baby back to her. *Everything happens for a reason, and that's a fact. God must really have had a reason for making Jared a widower, leaving him with an infant to love and to care for.*

Time is indeed a great healer. With time, Jacques should be a master of her own destiny. Her callings will lead and guide her, hopefully, keep her on the right track. Jared loved what **Chizitelụ** stood for. He chose to make it Jacque's middle name. It wouldn't be long before he nicknamed his one and only child **Chichi**.

Chapter 14

THE CRAVING: SWEET AND SOUR

The joy for many women comes with the birth of a child, especially their first time at being a mother. Many women have been blessed with the fruit of the womb, although some women haven't been so lucky at child-bearing. Motherhood is what completes most women. As women, we crave it. This yearning is only there by nature.

For years, **Chinazọ (God saves)** sat in the relative safety and comfort of her home wondering why she hadn't taken in. Her husband **Nnaemeka**, *aka* **Emeka (God has done it)**, had held back a secret he should have shared with her. He was actually the reason behind her implied barrenness. Years before he married her, Emeka was engaged to be married to his high school sweetheart. They had an unplanned pregnancy, and as a consequence, Emeka hurriedly married her. Unfortunately, she and her baby died during labor. The trauma of it hadn't left Emeka and nothing he did to shed the terrible memory from his mind worked. The experience had left him in perpetual fear of having another baby and possibly losing it. Because of that, he underwent a procedure that would prevent him from impregnating another woman.

Years into his marriage to Chinazọ, Emeka could no longer bear to see his wife's craving morph into repeated prolonged drifts of emotional pain and anguish for the both of them. Of course, he suffered more when those moments arrived. Because of that, he was forced to reverse the vasectomy he had done.

With the procedure reversed, Emeka rode home one night like he was the Aga Khan… you know, the Sultan of Brunei. He was ready for his wife. Chinazọ was lost in his brand of excitement. She had no way of knowing that the check he had put on hold had been cashed, and that on this night, she would be the recipient.

Emeka held nothing back on this night. A couple of months later, the result of this night's escapade could no longer be hidden from the naked eyes. Chinazor was pregnant. Her joy was in overdrive for the duration of the pregnancy. Only Chinazọ had no idea what was waiting for her in the next bend. Her joy and gladness was going to be short-lived, now that her pregnancy was in the nineth month.

If one has not physically experienced labor pains, one cannot begin to comprehend it. It is unfathomable. The depth of it couldn't be measured on any scale. For anyone to understand this kind of pain, one would have to live it. A woman in labor is like a woman scorned; she alone knows and owns the pain. When Chinazọ went into labor, the joy she had owned vanished, and the once mild-mannered, clean-mouthed housewife turned into an angry polecat. She shouted her displeasure at the entire pregnancy thing, rebuking her husband and his temerity at impregnanating her. *You have fooled me*, she hollered, each time the surge of pain passed through her body. She believed she had been abandoned, and made to bear the brunt of his gratuity.

Moments later, Chinazọ's face was lit; when she had her baby. The joy she had lived with returned. Her husband was no longer the monster. Even the nurses and the attending Physician were all amiable to her and she would, she said, come back for a second round, God willing.

CHAPTER 15
LOVE: THE JOURNEY OF LIFE

Love is the key that unlocks the beauty in each of us, if and when we let it. Let me take you on the journey of a young man named **Obiajụlụm** *aka* **Obi. Obiajụlụm (My heart is at peace)**.

Obi had a throng of female admirers as followers. He was tall and handsome, which caused young adult women to come after him like a school of fish. These women didn't mind his flaws. He was an amazing, smart young man. One would say that God created him on a Monday morning, after a restful weekend. His heart was as beautiful as he looked. He would be the first to tell you that he wasn't an alpha male. He was humble. Older women liked him too, not for themselves, but for their daughters. Obi, as the saying goes, '…had a good head on his shoulders.'

Obi was the only child of a wealthy king. The heir to the throne had just turned twenty-one. It should be noted that his mother died while giving birth to him. His father, the king, did not remarry. He did so to honor his dead wife and to devote his love totally to his son. The king would someday remarry. But he would have to wait for his son, Obi to get older before he took on a new wife.

That day finally came. While his son was basking in the glow of early manhood, the king got hitched. He married a woman much younger than he was. In the African way of thinking, it is highly appropriate that men be older than their spouses, even by decades. A few of years later, his new wife bore him three daughters in quick succession. Though the age gap between Obi and his sisters was wide, Obi was very happy to have siblings to love and share his life with.

Obi's mind was made up; he would travel around the world. It was the only way to keep his rioting desire to see the world in check. He believed the adventure would help him determine his destiny. Even his father thought so too. Right after the Christmas holiday was over, Obi set out on his journey.

He toured one country at a time, stayed in different cities before moving on to the next. Obi visited North America (United States and Canada), South America (Brazil), Europe (England; London, Paris, Italy, Russia, Germany, and Spain). He loved all these countries for different reasons. But, he had one city and one country in mind; the city of Berlin in Germany. He decided to go back to Germany to explore further.

Two days after he returned to Germany, Obi knew he had found the country to call home away from home. He applied to one of the top universities in Berlin. He was accepted into the College of Medicine. He took a year studying Deutsch. By the twelvth month, he was proficient enough to continue with his studies.

Everything from that moment on went smoothly. A few years later, the young man graduated with honors. That same year, right after graduation, Obi met Gabrielle; a young German heiress, and fell in love.

Meeting and then falling in love was one thing; but falling in love with a blue blood German was another. It could have been what turned his life around for the worse. Obi never calculated the risks he might be facing for getting hitched to an heiress most eligible German men were gunning for. The community was abuzz with the understanding that Gabrielle had found her love. But when the love she had found was the neanthethal African who spoke in *Umugumuga,* all hell broke loose. The younger German males in the community became especially envious of Obi, and had silently begun to demand that he back off Gabrielle or face their wrath.

Gabrielle's family was very wealthy and also well educated. They accepted and blessed their daughter's relationship with Obi. The family was happy Obi had graduated with honors to practice medicine. They saw that both Obi and Gabriele were genuinely in love and that they cared for each other. And the fact that Obi spoke fluent German was all the more reason they believed he'd stay in the country because he'd fit right in.

Months later, Obi took Gabrielle to his hometown in Nigeria to his father, and introduced her as the woman he had chosen to marry. His father was very pleased with Obi. His siblings were excited for him too. Gabrielle was definitely the right girl to take home to mama. Obi and Gabrielle were joined in holy matrimony in Lagos, Nigeria, one week after their traditional marriage ceremony.

Gabrielle also wanted a different kind of wedding.This second royal pageantry should cap things off. There was a good chance that the proposed second outing; the ceremonial blessing of the union in Germany was for the German people, and more so for her parents, who missed the first one in Lagos. Gabrielle's real reason for proposing this was not just to honor her parents, but as a way of making known to every German that she was married.

In the first three years of their marriage, Gabrielle and Obi were as happy as they could be. Not long after that, they were blessed with a baby girl. She was named **Ụzọamaka (Blessed path).** The baby's name signified the beauty of her father's long journey to Berlin.

Everything seemed to be traveling on a smooth path. Obi had gone further to train as a specialist in brain surgery. He became an accomplished Neurosurgeon. Gabrielle had also graduated from the same university with a degree in Software Engineering. They were living a very simple life, despite their elite backgrounds. Gabrielle conceived another child the same month Uzoamaka turned two. Obi and Gabrielle were thankful. There were frequent visits to Nigeria. These trips were made to expose Ụzọamaka to the Igbo culture.

One evening, Obi had planned a romantic outing with his pregnant wife. While he was rushing home early from work, he was ambushed, and was taken to a deserted building by unknown assailants. The assailants were three young German men who had been against Obi's marriage to Gabrielle. These men felt that Obi, a Negro, did not deserve to have Gabrielle as his wife. She was one of Berlin's most fascinating women any German male could have had for his wife. The passing of time had not, and did not do anything to amend the hearts of these haters. The creeps were still furious. It was clear that racism played a major role in the ordeal Obi suffered at the hands of these men.

Dr. Obi was missing, and he had been missing for days now. His family was turned upside down as they searched for him. This couldn't have happened at a worse time. Gabrielle's was unable to contain the ravages brought upon her because of the abduction. With the baby growing in her, her situation got worse. She became depressed, and her blood pressure went up. Worst of all, she had lost her appetite for food.

Obi's father flew to Berlin when news of his son's abduction reached him. The Police were alerted. The search had started. And, Obi still hadn't been found. There had not been any ransome made for Obi's return. With that, all hope of finding him was not lost.

Two weeks into his disappearance, a note finally arrived, demanding that Obi go back to Nigeria, minus his wife, Gabrielle. There was more; the abductors wanted Obi to leave Berlin without Gabrielle. They had severely beaten him, threatened him with death, if after his release, he stayed one day longer in Germany. Gabrielle was a big part of his life. Leaving her behind in Germany would be tantamount to losing a big part of him. He despised the idea. So, he told his kidnappers that he would not be leaving his family behind.

They tortured him some more. This time they applied other forms of torture that almost cost him his life. Obi was left for dead, in a pool of blood in an abandoned building.

It was day sixteen and Obi had not been found. Gabrielle was under so much pressure she was forced into labor in just thirty-four weeks. She was taken to the hospital immediately. As was expected, her blood pressure was high, and she had begun to spot, although not profusely. Her baby could be in danger, and her doctors thought an emergency Ceaseran-Section had to be performed to save her and her unborn child. It was a successful operation. Gabrielle and her baby were saved.

Back in the abandoned building, Obi was too frail, unable to scream or crawl his way out to seek help. His broken body was on the floor, in a putrid mixture of blood, urine, and feces. His life was on that precarious edge. It looked like only a miracle could save him from sudden death. *Miracles do happen when we least expect them.* Obi was going in and out of consciousness, not sure he would ever be rescued. Whenever his mind and consciousness would let him, he molded a prayer to hug his bruised lips. *Let someone find me, Dear God, Chukwu biko*!

Moments later, a mentally challenged homeless woman heard someone moaning in the abandoned building, and decided to take a look. She found Obi clinging on to life. She had no idea what to do; how to help the badly injured man. So totally confused, she watched Obi for a short time. Finally, she decided to help him. She started dragging his limp body out of the building. Finally, she pulled him to the roadside and left him there. Maybe someone would find him. Maybe Obi's life would be saved. Hours after he was left on the roadside, the Police found him.

Obi was rushed to the nearest hospital; the same hospital where Gabrielle had had her baby. He was unconscious when the Medics rolled him through the double doors leading into the emergency room. Neither Gabrielle nor any of his family members was aware that Obi had been rescued, and had been brought to the same hospital.

At the time Obi was rescued, he was not identifiable. They had no idea who the black man was. All they did was put together bits and pieces of physical information, in the hope they would get a match.

Many hours passed, Obi was still fighting for his life, and Gabrielle was still recovering from the trauma of childbirth.

But, Obi's father had been having some unexplained strange feelings.

While he was pacing the hospital halls, he noticed a bracelet on the floor. The bracelet looked familiar, so he picked it up. He immediately knew who the bracelet belonged to. He took it to the nurses, showed them what he had found in the hallway, and demanded to know where the man it belonged to was. A nurse took him to the room of the last patient the Medics had brought in a few hours ago. Obi's father broke down and cried, knowing it was his son the nurse had pointed out to him. He had given Obi the bracelet on his twenty-first birthday. But, it was unclear to him if his son was dead or alive.

It was Obi!

Father sat next to son for days. Although Obi was still in a coma, and didn't look like he would ever come out of it. His wife refused to be discharged until her husband recovered. In the midst of the unfolding tragedy, Obi's father pleaded with Gabrielle to allow him the honor to name his new grandson. She gladly obliged.

The older generations of Igbo men believe that every man needs a son to carry on the family name, from one generation to the next. He named his grandson, **Afamefuna (Let my lineage live on** or **May my name not be lost)**. He was afraid that he might lose his only son, even as he was hoping for a miracle.

Gabrielle was discharged with her baby after it was clear that Obi would survive. She had no choice, but to go home for the sake of her newborn. However, she was at the hospital every day, holding Obi's hand, loving him, and praying for the best. Four weeks later, she decided to take the baby to meet his father. While sitting next to Obi, Gabrielle implored on God to spare her husband's life. "Do not give me one life and take the other from me," she pleaded with God, with the baby in her arms.

She did this everyday; she would come and sit by his bedside at the break of dawn, and never left until after sunset. Sometimes, she and the baby would fall asleep, lying next to Obi, on his hospital bed. The scene was saturated with love and care, and the nurses who witnessed this phenomenon, sobbed at the spectacle.

By the fourth day, an hour into her visit, she felt fingers running through her hair. Startled! She looked up, and saw Obi looking at her. Her eyes were brimming with tears. She held him as long as she could, before rushing out to alert the hospital staff.

Life happened!

Obi came back from the *snares of the fowler and the noisome pestilence.* It was not his time to die. God may have decided to grant Obi with a second chance at life.

Obi's father was thrilled. He sang songs of praise to God, blessed his daughter-in-law and family for the extraordinary love they had shown to his son. He gave Gabrielle a name that could only be appropriate for a woman like her. He called her, **Akaraka diya (Her husband's destiny)**.

Obi was finally home with his family. After months of investigation, Obi's assailants were caught and brought to justice.

CHAPTER 16

HOPE, FAITH, AND LOVE

This story is about **Golibe (Rejoice)**. Golibe had a good heart, but had had a hard life and some very bad luck to go with it. She loved and cared for everyone around her, fed the hungry, clothed the homeless, and consoled the sorrowful, wherever she could find them. The woman was simply amazing, only her heart was empty because she yearned to be loved and cared for.

Not long after her last birthday, she met and fell in love with a man. After a short courtship, her heart fell in line with her feelings; she adored and took care of him. The least he did was to offer her his promisory hand in marriage. Few years later, he kept his other promises he had made to her; vacations to far and distant lands. The courtship was written and designed in heaven, Golibe believed. She gladly accepted his stupendous offers, and allowed herself to be carried to places her mind could construct; hoping at all times that this love that had found her would last a lifetime. Golibe's life's goal was being fulfilled, and she wasn't in any kind of dream. The possibility of a marriage, and the type of care she thought she could never own had touched her.

But, there was an aspect of her past life gnawing at her soul. She had lived a reckless life at one time, and had gone through series of abortions, some of them botched. Golibe was afraid she would never be able to conceive again. Approximately seven weeks after her engagement, she found out that she was pregnant. Her fears left her as she cowered in supplication to God and His miraculous gift of love. Golibe was 32 years old at the time and for her, all hope of having a normal life was a fairytale. And now, this sudden thrust of fresh, vibrant shower she had been made to bathe in: *This joy of endless contentment that caressed her spirit*, she prayed, should never cease.

We make plans and hope for the best. Sometimes, it is the worst that rears up.

Eight weeks into her pregnancy, the worst happened. Golibe's fiancé dropped the bomb. He decided that he had had enough, and would rather not be in the relationship. No reason was given. She was left in the dark to decipher the mystery of his sudden departure from the unbroken bliss they had shared. The man was on a roll… he also didn't want anything to do with his unborn child. Here, a reason was given. Simply put, he was not ready to be a father. Right then, Golibe's life had shifted, following a predictable trajectory that would eventually smother her. She was heartbroken to say the least.

Severe stress contributes to a chemical imbalance in our bodies. Golibe's body was stressed to a breaking point, and of course, a few weeks later, she had a miscarriage that had been waiting to happen. As if to make her situation worse, her doctor informed her that her womb had weakened considerably, and that she may not be able to conceive another child. *Imagine the state of mind Golibe was in.* She stared at the doctor speechless, and with catatonic eyes. Moments later, she left her doctor's office, ambled away like a zombie, her dear heart in her hand. But, she hadn't lost it all; she went to a nearby lake to meditate. There, she cried endlessly while having a conversation with God.

God hears and sees it all…

Weeks later, she cut her losses, focused on her blessings and tried to move on with her life. Her only chance at being a mother had ended abruptly. But, that didn't stop her from getting involved in her community. Her mind was made up; she decided she'd continue being a blessing to other people… something she was cut out to be. Only this time, she redirected her mission, focusing on a particular motherless babies' home. Golibe supported the home financially, and also devoted a lot of her time caring for the children at the home.

Two years later, she thought about taking a vacation. One morning, after her usual cup of iced coffee, she decided the trip had to happen. Only she didn't have a place in the whole wide world locked away in her heart. Golibe parked her bags and headed for the airport anyway, hoping that somehow, somewhere in the elusive vastness of the western United States would eventually make her mind up for her. Just as she stepped out of the cab at the airport, her mind was seeing stunning topographical vistas that defined Palm Springs, California. Golibe bought a ticket to Palm Springs, took a seat in the airport lobby to wait for her flight.

Just before boarding time, a voice broke behind her.

"Hello."

The voice was rich; a blend of nimble contralto and mild-mannered baritone. She looked up and saw a gorgeous man standing right behind her. Golibe stopped momentarily to gauge the man's esquisite handsomeness, but more so, for his Zulu-like boldness, for standing too close to her. All he did was smile to assuage her fears. She responded to him by smiling narrowly, but kept on walking toward the boarding gate. When she turned again, the gentleman was gone. She muttered;

"That's strange."

Few hours later, Golibe arrived in Palm Springs. She was excited to be there. It was her first vacation in a long time. Only this time, her life was about to undergo another major change.

Her vacation started right after she got off the plane. She was picked up in a limousine and taken to an exotic resort and spa called '*Riviera Resort and Spa*.' It is a gorgeous place for beautiful events and for anyone looking for complete relaxation. Many have experienced the joy of being completely pampered in this beautiful hideaway.

She rented a beautiful suite overlooking the expansive blue waters of the Pacific. Golibe needed a breather, and this was it! Again, her life was about to be interrupted. Come dusk, she went down for dinner at the lounge. Dinner was served. While she was enjoying her meal, she heard a familiar voice; the voice that belonged to the man at the airport; *the vanishing-act specialist*, she had dubbed him. *What is he doing here*? Had he been following her? And what's with his voice that would cause her ear drums to roll and rumble in harmonious crackle? Her senses were heightened, implying that he could be closer to her than he had been at the airport. She looked up, knowing it was him; the same gorgeous looking gentleman! Her face lit up. She felt like a teenager, and then tried to look away from him. But his eyes held her prisoner. The smile on his face encouraged her. It gave her unusual kind of warmth. Golibe fell back into her chair, as if to abandon her dinner.

"My table is larger… I mean, cozier… would you… that is…?

Even in all his debonair looks, he was fighting the willies. The man wasn't without fear, after all. Why not? He knew he was playing a game of depthless uncertainty with the most beautiful woman he had ever seen… and he could lose.

She knew what he wanted. *He wants an evening with me, is that it*? She asked herself. Golibe would rather not stop him. *Go ahead ask me for an evening out, Teddy Pendagrass*, she cooed, nearly giving her thoughts away. *If you are wishing for a quick answer, go ahead, ask me, I'll make your boldness pay off. Oh yes…* it was the voice, *stupid*!

He asked her again, this time with deeper resonance.

Golibe got up before the stranger had finished with his request. She thrust her hand out. He took it gently, squeezing, without making it obvious.

"My name's Styga… Bruce Styga"

Screw Teddy! Golibe thought. *Your name has timber*, she concluded.

"I am Golibe," she said smiling, to catch up with the moment.

He smiled some more to warm her up.

"My table boasts of clear water from the artic, and a bottle of wine from the Swiss side of the Alps."

"The Alpine red is what my taste buds are craving for."

It was the beginning of a great friendship.

Golibe and Bruce lived in the same city, both learned. They hurried their dinner and drove off in his rented car. Thirteen months later, Golibe and Bruce were still great friends. Actually, they had become soulmates. Not long after that, subsequent trips were taken as their love for each other grew. Bruce was mostly the initiator; he would construct activities he knew would blow her mind, and then invite her to lavish in its luxury. He saw through the window of her heart; what it was she needed. It was from there he strumped the harp to set her on fire, all at his own volition. He embraced the totality of her being, and had no doubts he would die for her. Golibe probably felt exactly the same for Bruce.

Bruce had been married when he was twenty-five years old. He was blessed with two sons. His marriage ended because his wife was unfaithful a few times. Bruce could not accept these betrayals, and he had no choice but to end his ten-year marriage. He had vowed not to give his heart to another woman. Well… as the Monkees would say: *And then I saw her face.*

Golibe was elated, but cautious. The remnants of her past experiences were still lingering before her eyes, like a swarm of butterflies. To an extent, Bruce was the same way; his own experiences weren't letting him be either. He was mortified by the sheer belief that most women out there are potential cheats. But somehow, with Golibe, her aura was doing a great job rewriting the scary quotients in his beliefs. They could have been made for each other; Golibe and Bruce, that is. They had the same fears, but had somehow shed them when their paths crossed. *Was it destiny that their paths crossed?*

It is the Writer's belief that Golibe and Bruce did not meet by chance. Their meeting was destined to happen when it did. Bruce was aware that Golibe had had trouble in the past conceiving. He was planning on marrying her anyway, even as he believed she could still have difficulties conceiving. Not long after he proposed to her, they returned to Palm Springs and got married.

Golibe and Bruce were reborn in love. Their hearts were in sync; humming the same melody of a song. They accepted each other's flaws and focused on both of their strengths; complimenting each other in the process. Their love was the perfect example of the true meaning of love.

Four years after her marriage to Bruce, Golibe was still childless. One day, after she and her husband had shared a pot of coffee, Golibe suddenly took a turn for the worse; she fell very sick.

Bruce took her to the hospital. The doctors didn't let her go. Rather, they kept her for a few more days. Bruce was saddened because they could not determine what was wrong with Golibe. She reminded Bruce that they had no choice, but to submit everything to God. On the second day, the doctors ran more tests. Finally, they had an answer for both man and wife.

"Mr. and Mrs. Styga, you are eight weeks pregnant," the doctor said.

Golibe was truly pregnant. The moment in the hospital room could have been doused with icy cold water. Time itself was under lockdown; frozen. The live hearts in the room were audible in their respective beats; you could hear them… tick, tock, tick, tock, just like the tintinnabulation coming from the wall clock. And for those things that moved, they did so in slow motion ritual. Then, the veil was lifted the moment Golibe laughed; she had then heard what the doctor had said moments ago.

"From your mouth to God's ears," Golibe said.

Bruce got up, stood in the doctor's face and dared him to repeat himself.

How amazing is the grace of God? Amazing!!! God is never late. He shows up when the time is right and when He does, His hand print is marked.

Thirty-two weeks came so fast and the babies were ready to meet mommy and daddy. After five hours of labor, identical female twins were born.

Life is indeed a journey. It has been so for this family. Golibe and Bruce gave their twins names that would uplift the name of God: **Chisomebi (God lives with me)** and **KọdiliChukwu (It is up to God)**.

When all hope is gone, remember that life is hope. And, as long as we have the gift of life, then, there is hope for a better tomorrow. We must also remember that the gift of love is the gift of giving. When you give (sow seed) without expectation, there is a reward from God.

CHAPTER 17
ALMOST LIKE 'SARAH'

"Age is mind over matter. If you don't mind, it doesn't matter," Satchel Page; the great Negro League Baseball player. True, a woman's biological clock ticks with time. When choices are made, they are made for different reasons. So, what works for Janet may or may not work for Jane! It is that simple.

Ginika (Full name is **GinikaChukwu** meaning: **What is greater than God?**) had an idea of what her perfect man should look like and be like. She had forgotten, or rather ignored the fact that no man alive could fill that bill, at least, not since He came and went. Yes, we know that it is only God who is the only perfect Being. She wanted and needed her man to look a certain way, behave in a certain way, and definitely have deep pockets. There is nothing wrong with that. Ginika was adamant, and would not relent on the kind of man she deemed was suitable for her.

Time was running out for Ginika, and she knew it. That didn't stop her from turning down as many suitors as she could. Her reason was that none of the men had the mental acquity she was hoping for nor had any of them shown her that he possessed that delicate splash of inner beauty; something most ordinary women couldn't even detect when they saw it.

For years, she was the hottest 'diva' on the block. With time, all the available suitors were married off. Ginika woke up one morning and realized that there was a chance she could spend the rest of her life, a lonely woman. She had turned forty-six years just a couple of days ago, and the erstwhile beautiful young woman she saw in the mirror daily had somehow been vanishing with time. As the days rolled by, she was reluctant looking into the same mirror she had owned for more than a dozen years. On the days the courage was there to look, she saw she had begun to shrivel as would any aging goddess. Even as a successful career woman, most eligible men saw her past her prime and would not engage her in any kind of small talk about matters of the heart.

Meanwhile, Ginika was no virgin, and she had been around the block a few times. Her playbook was old and out of fashion, and it was too late to mount any kind of strategy that would rewrite her luck with men. With her good taste in food and clothing, she could only go so far. The men that noticed her were in a hurry to back off after a quick roll in the sack. To make matters worse, she was no longer of child-bearing age. Her daily dose of happiness began to diminish. Her public appearances suffered too. Ginika had become a recluse without knowing it. Behind closed doors, she would break down and weep, realizing how lonely she was. She wished she could change things around; her age for starters, to give herself another chance at being a married woman.

Though her biological clock was ticking as loud as the clock on Times Square, she could only hope to be a mother someday, even if she couldn't find lasting love. She had started looking at adopting a child to fill the void in her life.

Ginika woke up one early Saturday morning with her mind made up; she would adopt a baby. She went to an adoption agency to fill out the necessary paperwork. Six weeks later, after all the requirements were met, Ginika adopted a two-week old baby girl. She named her **Chikọdili** (**It is up to God**). Her life had returned to normal again. Now a happy woman and mother, she had reconstructed her dreary life into something of great value and excitement. She rejoined the life she had abandoned. Ginika picked up her career from where she had dumped it, and proceeded almost faultlessly.

As the years went by, mother and daughter had bonded. *The two became one happy family.* She had come to realize that she did not need a man to complete her. There are those that would rely on a man to be the sole source of their happiness. *When you give another individual the power to control your life, you risk the possibility of ever having a happy life.* That was why Ginika upped and adopted Chikọdili. Love, she realized, could be found without much effort, in the most unlikely of places. For sure, one doesn't have to be married to be fulfilled.

Ginika lived life one day at a time. Now, she was grateful for what she was blessed with. She had come to the realization that something good could come to anyone when one least expected it. Time and chance passed

Ginika for different reasons. Maybe for her, it was the way it was meant to be; to lead her to the life she was truly destined to have.

She was given the chance to experience love through Chikọdili, and she took it. If it was ever meant to be, the man of her dreams could still be out there, and who knows, might someday walk into her life.

CHAPTER 18

WHEN THREE BECOMES ONE...

Most African countries do not frown at polygamy, and most practice it. Being a polygamist is a choice. However, being a product of polygamy is not by choice. In today's Africa, one decides to take more than one wife either because of social status and/or financial wherewithal. Royalty is no longer a factor. A poor man can decide to marry more than one wife because he feels like it. In the old days, having more than one wife was one of the perks of being born into royalty. It is okay for a king (An **Igwe**) to take more than one wife if it pleases him. More still, he could keep and maintain concubines outside his home. Polygamy has its many facets, and the hassles are just as plentiful as you would find in the household of one who is married to one woman.

Nnamdi (My Father/God lives) was not a king. He was ignorant, as well as being arrogantly wealthy. And he wasn't the kind of man to marry one woman. He married three women in quick succession, as a way of managing his ego. They all lived in his big house.

Everything about this man had to be about numbers, big numbers, that's it! He made sure his wives had five children each. But, the only thing he couldn't control was the sex of each child. If he were able to rewrite the male/female quotient, during or after every intimacy, he would have done so.

When a man decides to take a wife, it is usually a big step. He may never understand the woman he had married, even how her thought processes float with each situation. Her thought processes could follow a trajectory that he might never be able slow down, or make sense of. What any man stands the chance of doing is to bring into his house as his wife, an extraterrestial in human form and not know it. It all begins with that absurdness in strangeness, in all matters that would otherwise have demanded a shot of common sense. But, the bad wife would likely take the issue into far-out territories as a way of making sure the issue remained unresolved. At this point, both parties had drifted into different orbits. It would be up to one of them to catch the reins and stop the free fall.

You see, for the first time, both man and wife are forced to make adjustments to accommodate the other. Now, you have probably gotten the picture; what the man with multiple wives could be faced with. Being with one partner is tasking. But, when one had bitten off more than one could chew, the jaws are flared and become painful. But, for Nnamdi, the number of wives determines a man's social status.

Don't forget that marriage is like a packaged gift. *Only, it is in no way a gift.* The recipients are usually unaware of the content until it is unwrapped. What one finds could be empty, or only loaded with potentially explosive gunpowder.

Nnamdi was aware of the chaos and squabbles in his household. His many wives couldn't have stopped him from philandering. They knew he had concubines and secretly prayed he didn't increase their fold to a half dozen.

'My concubines make me whole,' he once told an elder in his village.

A good number of men, young and old, believe that once they can provide the basic necessities for their families, then they are within their rights to find extra pleasure wherever they can find it. It was what Nnamdi believed in. He provided for his harem, and was therefore free to seek other pastures, and graze in wild spheres.

Nnamdi had his shortcomings. He was incapable of loving his many wives the way he should. He chose one, the third wife, and actually fell in love with her. With this wife, Nnamdi exchanged vows, and just like that, it had begun to look like the rest of his wives were intruders in the home they all shared. Sending all his wives away just to be with the one he had chosen would have been an abomination. He didn't know it, but he was the the architect of his own misery, all because of his one bad decision.

This third wife, Mabel, was undoubtedly the prettiest. She was humble too. Naturally, the other wives were envious of Mabel's beauty and their husband's love for her. Mable knew her goose could be cooked when she became the chosen one. She had nothing in her arsenal to thwart the tomahawks; the co-wives (**ndi nwuyedi**) who were hurling her way.

When one's conscience is clear, one fears no allegation. *You trust God; He fights for you.*

Mabel named her first son **Chinedum**, meaning **God leads me**. When the second child came, she named her **Chimdinma (My God is good).** And the last child, another girl, was named **Chimdaalụ (Thank you, my God**).

The other wives detested the names Mable had given her children, and were undoubtedly recoiling with envy. It didn't take long, and the cauldron had begun to simmer; the other wives hatched evil plots against Mabel and her children.

Mabel suspected she was under fire and quickly submitted all her fears and supplications to God. The other wives poisoned the hearts of their children against Mabel's children. Nnamdi's family was divided into two factions. Not all the children were in on the plot. But, there were those of them that followed in their mother's plan to bring harm to Mabel and her offsprings.

Nnamdi had no choice, but called his family together for a meeting. He made everyone swear by the bible that no one would do any harm to the other. Many of them; the evil plotters refused to swear by the holy book. Mabel, her three children, and some of the other children agreed to the terms of the meeting. But, it didn't stop the other women from going ahead with their evil plan.

Few weeks later, one of the children told their father of the plot their mothers had cooked up. It was confirmed that Nnamdi's two other wives were planning to kill Mabel with her children by way of black magic. If that did not work, they had an option; employ assassins to do the job. Mabel believed that her God fought for her and her children. No one knew for sure how it all went down, but the hatred for Mabel and her children spilled over. The evil-plotting wives were exhausted. They had failed in all of their efforts. The wives finally came out and made searing, mind-numbing confessions.

On this basis, the elders of the land agreed with Nnamdi that his two conniving wives would leave his home, and be banished for a long period of time. Days after the wives were exposed in their plot; the village elders sent them packing.

Mabel pleaded with her husband and the elders to be compassionate and forgive the wives. Their behavior was an abomination in the eyes of God and man. Nnamdi had no choice in the matter; he denounced the two wives for behaving so brazenly.

Mabel became Nnamdi's only wife. She took care of all the children the banished women had inadvertently left in her care. Nnamdi stopped his dangerous liaisons with the concubines he had littered around the village. He focused his time and love on his wife and children. Mabel received more blessings; she bore Nnamdi two more children.

Chapter 19

THE CHAMELEON "OGWUMAGANA"

He said. She said. The truth is with him. And the truth is with her. Regardless of the face value of a coin or a story, it is what it is. We all have different faces, names, and our lives move in different directions. But we all have one thing in common; our conscience. A coin has two sides, and for a good reason. The same is true with the events in our lives and the stories we tell. Still, regardless of our side of the story, the truth unfolds eventually.

There is an Igbo saying, **Adighi ezo afọ ime ezo, (Pregnancy cannot be concealed)**. If carried to term, the baby will eventually be born, and the truth will be known. It is clear that one cannot run from the truth regardless of which side of the coin your story is on. Nevertheless, when truth is hidden, the lips may lie, but the heart knows.

In most of life's compelling stories, there could be two or more sides. The circumstances could be similar, exact or completely different. Although a fraction of the stories could sound similar, but it is these little bits and pieces that could be in the way, generate different speculations and interests when the story is told.

Chinedum (God leads me) *aka* **Edu** had two wives, **BelụChi (Only God)** and **IfụnanyaChi (God's love)** *aka* **Ify.** Edu loved both of his wives with the same equanimity.

When a man takes on a second wife, most times, jealousy darkens the morning sun. Edu was a peaceful and fair man. He married BelụChi first, and they were blessed with a female child. Four years later, BelụChi was still unable to conceive another child. Man and wife decided they will take on another wife. It was a mutual agreement, Edu believed.

Ify's bride price was paid and the traditional marriage followed thereafter. BeluChi welcomed her husband's new wife; her **nwunye di** into her new home. She opened her heart and embraced her. Ify was happy and felt right at home.

It is wise to be cautious when you tread on unfamiliar territory. The Igbos say; 'It is better to stand on one leg until you familiarize yourself with your new surroundings, before you lower the other leg.' Ify had failed to do this, and had stamped both feet down with overly embellished confidence. She was so comfortable; she was blind to the obvious facts of jealousy lurking in the place she called home.

After two years, Ify had not conceived a child for her husband. Because of this, the situation in the house got colder and meaner. BeluChi had an opening; she blamed their husband, for making her agree to such a stupid decision to marry a second wife. *Delay of blessing does not imply denial.* A few months later, Ify became pregnant. When delivery time came, she gave birth to a baby girl. Her husband was not so thrilled because he wanted a male child that would carry on his name. To him, his reason for marrying a second wife hadn't been realized. BeluChi was happy for the obvious reason; Ify could not give their husband what she also could not give him. Ify was grateful to God nonetheless. She named her baby, KeleChi (**Thank God**) *aka* **Chi.**

Chi was seven months old when her mother, Ify conceived another child. Her husband prayed for a son, BeluChi prayed for a girl, while Ify prayed for the "Will of God to prevail." Time came so fast and passed! She had a son. Edu could not have been happier. His heart was full of gratitude to God for this grace. The first son of the family was named **Obinna**, meaning **The Father's heart** *aka* **Obi**. The naming ceremony/Christening for Obi was indeed festive. Edu bragged about his son everywhere he went. He was a proud father. Meanwhile, BeluChi was raging with jealousy, but she hid it well.

One hot Sunday afternoon, few weeks after Obi's naming ceremony had passed; things began to change for the worse. The baby was being bottle-fed by his mother, when BeluChi asked if she could help feed the baby. Ify was happy and saw no reason to deny her. So, she gracefully obliged.

What happened next was beyond comprehension. During the exchange of the baby, Ify believed that her son was safely in the hands of BeluChi. In the next breath, she saw her baby boy fall through the hands BeluChi had stretched out to receive him. The sickening thud heard when the two-month old baby hit the concrete floor would forever be etched in Ify's mind.

There was no cry from the baby, signifying that the infant could be seriously injured or dead. Ify screamed. BelụChi sneered. All hell broke loose. It looked like there was a death in the family. Her screams were unmatched, vehement, and boundless in its volumn. People had begun to arrive in droves, to see what was happening in Edu's home.

BelụChi was quick on her feet. She told a harried story that was far from the truth. She fabricated a yarn to her listeners, including her husband.

"Ify had complained of exhaustion from being up all night with the baby," BelụChi had said. "She confided in me, telling me that she was on the verge of a break down." She insinuated that Ify had dropped the baby while sleeping on the couch.

Ify was overwhelmed by the sight of her seemingly lifeless baby, and may not have heard what BelụChi had said in her defense.

BelụChi was lying, obviously. Ify's heart was racing. Her face was soaked in tears. She held her son so tight and cried to the Heavens for help. She knew rushing her baby to the hospital was meaningless. The inadequacy of healthcare services in most of the hospitals in Nigeria is not a joke. If that were to be the only way to save her baby, her boy would definitely die.

The pain she was feeling exacerbated. People had started calling her names. They called her a witch. Their collective voices could have come from hell, as in a cacophonous dirge. Ify managed to ignore them. She held her baby, kissed him, hoping to feel his breath. With hope slipping, she lifted her voice to the Heavens, calling on the God she worshipped, to spare her son.

This was the song she sang to her Father in Heaven:

'Chukwu a gọzigo akara aka m (God has blessed my destiny).

Who am I? I do not deserve your grace.

Yet, you blessed me.

You showered me with your grace.

Ebube elu igwe mara mma (The wonders of the Heavens are beautiful).

The way you bless me amazes my enemies.

Chi mụ (My God),

Please fill Obinna's lungs with your breath of life.

Mgbe mụ na-asụ ude na-abali (When I dwelled in misery and hopelessness at night),

Enweghi onye na-ajụ mụ ese (No one came to my aid)

Chi ewere la ụtụtụ jie (Day has turned into darkness, in broad light).

If my destiny was up to the world, I know I would not be blessed.

Lord, you have blessed me

I thank you for my son.

Be gracious and wipe my tears.'

This song was what sustained her in the midst of the verbal abuse she got from some of the neighbors. She continued to speak and pray life into her son's body.

BelụChi's tongue was still running freely with her lies. Her husband stood speechless in horror. He was in a state of shock. While Ify was still holding their son, singing and praying, he quickly walked towards Ify and joined her in prayers. They both laid hands on their son and prayed harder. The baby seemed so lifeless.

Minutes later, the baby's closed eyes moved. His hands twitched. The life in him was being rebooted. Then, the cry came. The scene froze up. Ify, unable to contain her imploding joy screamed again. Someone hollered: *Who said miracles do not happen o?*

Ify, still in tears, exclaimed:

"Chi m ọma, odogwu na-agha, ọ bụ gi na-enye ndụ, ekele diri gi!" (My good God, Mighty Warrior, you are the one who gives life. All honor and glory belong to you).

Indeed, God shows up when all hope is lost.

Ify, her husband, and everyone in the room were in shock, screaming in amazement, except for BelụChi. She left the room in a rush. It was time for BelụChi to run for her life, literally. She disappeared before anyone noticed that she was gone. Remember that God never likes ugly.

THINK NO EVIL: HEAR NO EVIL: SEE NO EVIL: DO NO EVIL.

CHAPTER 20

'TO BE OR NOT TO BE...'

C**hekwube** (**Rely on God**) lived in the big city with her husband, **Echezọna** (Full name: **EchezọnaChi** meaning: **Do not forget God**). This same husband was also married to **Ngọzi** (**Blessing**). Ngọzi was Echezona's first wife, only she had been unable to conceive a child for him. He was forced to marry Chekwube as his second wife, to try and change his luck with barrenness.

Not long after he took a second wife, three months to be exact, Chekwube became pregnant. Echezọna was thrilled and grateful to God. Ngọzi was having a difficult time wondering why God had not extended His blessings to include her. She was not jealous of Chekwube. She actually helped Chekwube during the entire time she was pregnant.

Months later, **Chizitelụm (God brought me**) was born, and the family could not have been happier. There was a naming ceremony conducted two months after the baby arrived. And as always, everyone they knew was invited. She was named after her paternal grandmother. The event lasted an entire day, exactly the way Echezọna wanted it.

Chizitelụm had the blessing of living in a loving home. She had everything, plus three parents that really cared for her. Everyone loved to cuddle her, especially during feeding times. At five years old, she had grown to be cheerful and even more beautiful.

Chekwube never knew nor understood the extent of Ngọzi's love for her child. It had begun to bother her that Ngozi, who was without a child, would love and care for Chizitelụm the way she did.

Chekwube was now on the war path to protect her turf and what she had perceived could be a threat to the well-being of her child. She had crafted in her mind an implied, but diabolic plot that Ngozi had to be hatching to destroy her and her daughter. She took the plot to her husband and explained it thus:

THE WAY THEY SAW IT

Echezọna listened with rapt attention at the tale of a brewing murder scheme Ngọzi was supposedly hatching. Chekwube added color to her story, embellishing the so-called Ngọzi's plot to eliminate Chekwube, so she could adopt Chizitelụm, and live happily ever after with Echezọna.

"Nonsense…!" Echezọna screamed.

Chekwube knew what buttons to push to get her husband eating from the palm of her hands. She reached and pulled out a plastic pouch containing brown powder; an extract of weird concoctions. She threw that at her husband.

"That's what I found in Ngọzi's room. That is ***Nchi-Che.*** You swallow a gram of that, and you are dead, **Nna mụ**." She stared at her husband for any kind of reaction. She got none, so she fired away.

"What do you think that stuff is doing in her room? Don't you think she is waiting for the right moment to slip it into our food, mine especially? Why would she want any us dead?" She screamed harder. "**Chukwu Nna ekwena! God forbid!** So you can't see it? Are you so blind that you can't see death crawling up in your bed as you sleep? **Nwokem, gee mụ nti**; listen to me. I am the one with a child for you. She is coming after me. She wants my baby. She wants me dead. Then, it will be you, the witch and our baby. That's her plan!"

Echezọna drifted into a mild state of hypnosis. He was actually feeling confused and angry at the same time. And because he was unable to manage both emotions, he became truly agitated; he shot up from his chair like a rocket leaving its pod, cursing, berating his first wife for her temerity. Chekwube urged him on, fueling his anger by conducting and orchestrating his demeaning diatribes against the first wife. The moment was ripe. The die was cast. Ngọzi would have no where to run to. She would have no defense to profer. Chekwube had a sly, mischievous smile on her face. And with Echezọna, the clouds of black plumes had descended on his home.

As he stormed out of his bedroom, Chekwube was right behind him. Ngọzi was in her bedroom knitting. She only looked up when her bedroom door fell off its hinges. Her benign countenance did not change. Ngọzi put down the crop of cloth she was working on and then spoke so softly and disarmingly.

"*Nna anyi*, do you have to come at me in anger?" Ngọzi asked.

"I want you to pack up and leave this house! Do you hear me?" Echezọna screamed.

"Have I done anything to annoy the only man I have ever loved? If it is so, please tell me what it is I have done to incur your anger, and I will say I am sorry."

"Woman, your days here with us are numbered. Pack up, now," Chekwube began to say. She was cut off.

"**Mechiee ọnụ gi**… Shut up your mouth," Echezọna barked at Chekwube, and then turned to face Ngọzi again. "I don't have to poison you to kill you, woman. I will do it with my hands and let the town know why it is so in my house," he said and stormed out again. Only this time, Chekwube remained behind. She was looking forward to throwing down her own gauntlet at Ngọzi.

"You are the woman from hell. **Amosu (witch)**! How did you figure you can kill me and take my child for yourself? **Ụsụkangwụ**" (bat, as in out of hell)!

Chekwube stormed out, leaving Ngọzi shredded up. Tears rolled. She coiled up in her bed and tried to ride it out by coaxing her weak body to go to sleep.

Two hours later, Ngọzi found the strength to step out of bed. She left her bedroom looking for her husband. How to explain to him that she had no knowledge of what he was talking about was the hard part. She knew Chekwube's hands were wrapped around the things she had been accused of. She gave up on her musings when it appeared no one was in the house with her. She wondered where they had gone. And then, the worst happened.

Echezọna came walking in through the front gate with Chizitelụm in his arms, both covered in blood. Ngọzi ran like the wind. Her husband was frozen stiff just as he cleared the double gates. Tears ran like a river from his eyes. Ngọzi approached both with the same caution as you would approach a wounded tiger.

"***Nna mụ* ọgini**? What is it?"

When Echezọna said nothing, she took the child from his arms, nudged her husband to start walking toward the house. Echezọna was speechless, and could still be staring at the proverbial ghost he had seen earlier. In the house, he sat down a little heavily on the couch, and then opened up in a retch. Ngọzi, the wise woman that she was, allowed him recovery time.

When he was spent, she stared at him, imploying him to tell her what had happened.

At the end of his emotional outpouring, her husband told her how he had stormed out of the house in anger. He was driving to a place where he, Chekwụbe and Chizitelụm would be alone. They didn't get there. He had plowed into an oncoming truck, when the car he was driving veered off its lane.

"Chekwube is dead!" he cried out.

Ngọzi began to sob uncontrollably. She was speechless while rocking the child in her arms and groaning in pain. Echezọna looked up once to observe her; her unpretentious outburst, the totality of her grief was unmistakably sincere. He began to cry some more. It was not clear where his grief was at the time, who or what was causing it. He began to sing a dirge, filled with his heartfelt apology for the way he had treated her. He pleaded with Ngọzi to forgive him and Chekwube.

"***Ilo bụ na ndụ...***!" He moaned. "Chekwube obviously made the story up about you. But I was stupid to have believed any of it. I know your spirit, my love, **biko** forgive me."

Things did change fast for Ngọzi. Exactly two years after the death of Chekwube, Ngọzi took in. She had a baby boy. She and Echezọna named him Chekwube, in memory of Echezọna's second wife.

CHAPTER 21

EZIGBO M: MY LOVE

IN THE BEGINNNING

The flight of the ducks rippled the lake. The trees were doing a slow dance. Joggers were around the lake. Picnickers snacked while the music played on. The air was simply crisp. It was the perfect season for that very reason. It all began by the Lake Shore. It is amazing how two hearts living separate lives could harmonize in almost perfect tune. He stood there like he had been waiting; waiting for her to show up. Well, she did show up. She was passionate about writing and had come to the lake to draw inspiration. Staring into the beautiful greenery that is the backdrop of the Lake does that for her.

It was not a coincidence that she chose this morning to visit the Lake. That precise moment was predestined for her. And this moment, it hung like a scud of bright clouds daring her to enter the trough. A good spot for meditation is always vast, pristine, calm, and removed from the ordinary. To scribble those beatific verses, she would have to be on her most creative plain. And for love to bloom, she would need the calm, blue waters before her to make all of that fall in place. So, she entered.

She lowered herself to sit, mindful of the dew-laden grass. That had never stopped her before. Her thoughts sprung that familiar spreadsheet; she must pick and choose where to anchor her thoughts this morning. But something else was rushing her, and the calmness she had come to seek came too soon. Her soul was ready to take flight. Why? The chills persisted and her hands went around her body to arrest the surge. She stopped for a moment to gauge the scene, and to figure if it was all real. Then, she raised her head, with her eyes shut. A few seconds later, those brown soft eyes slit open, taking the scene one bite at a time, searching the crop of trees in the distance, and then seeing the most amazing child-like face of a young man gazing back at her.

He came closer… he could have floated towards her, and said;

"Hello, my name is **Ọdiatụ** (**Pride and joy** (in the Lord)) *aka* **Ọdy**."

Like a teenage girl, she blushed and looked away, but managed to let the word slip through;

"Hi," she said, moving her eyes away from him, to douse his gaze.

Ọdy was a stranger, a very funny one, and shy to boot. He seemed coordinated and very polite. When she saw no threat about him, they talked for a little while. It was the beginning of an almost never-ending story; the story of one true love.

What they felt for each other was a rare gift in all the hidden treasures of life. They believed that their love was a miracle, and it had to be. To do nothing with the opportunity presented to them would have been a mistake. As far as they were both concerned, they were living in a world they had created for themselves: There was no one else out there for either of them to have loved and cherished. They loved each other without reservation. And in truth, this love could have completed their life's journey.

But wait!!!

Twelve months later, things changed for both of them.

Many nights, she would hug her bed, and would allow the thoughts of him to fill her body and soul. Her heart was glad, but it would be just for a moment: She wondered what he could be doing alone, without her around. Those were the moments she missed him. Almost everything she did each day was tinged with the memory of Ọdy. Every melody she heard was a melody of his sweetness, and she missed him even more. When he left her, she was heartbroken. She was quick to understand that he hadn't done that deliberately.

His laughter, although deep in its resonance, was music to her ears. God had to know about this creation of His, and she had had such conversations with The Father about him. How could he not have known how badly she would be hurting? How could He not have known how much she was missing him? Or how much she cared for him? Didn't Ọdy feel the emptiness in her heart when he left? He had seen through the window of her imperfect heart, yet he had embraced and loved her wholly. Ọdy had completed her. Now, when she reminisced about him, she would smile, and then cry wholesomely while imagining all that could have been.

ALMOST THE END

She wrote him a letter one moment in time…

"Ọdiatụ, ezigbo m,

It hurt me deeply to imagine the pain you must have felt in your last moments. When the heat from the fire burned, I imagined the tears of pain rolling down your angelic face. If only you had listened and not ride with your boys on that roadtrip. Now I realize that fate had other plans. On that fateful evening, without knowing that you had gone, I had prepared your favorite dish, waiting for you to come to me. I called your mobile phone severally, but you never answered. I needed to tell you how much I loved you; how happy I was looking forward to seeing you that night. I fell apart when I heard you were gone. In that moment, I could not breathe. My heart left my body. I could feel that precious life leaving your body at that precise moment.

You were granted no chance of bailing out of a terrible situation. And most of all, I was denied the chance to whisper to you how much I loved you. It's not okay, but I can manage it because I now understand that it was not up to you to have left me when you did. I pray that you are resting in the bosom of The Father. I will always love you. And I hope we get the chance to meet again. You will always be my ezigbo; my one and only love."

Sọniru

He had left for the great beyond without her consent. She had written an elegiacal tribute to her love, wishing he was just asleep, as in a wake-able slumber. Like that 'slices of death' sleep is. The great one, Edgar Allen Poe had talked about thus: 'Sleep, those little slices of death; oh how I loathe them.'

'*To die, to sleep; To sleep: perchance to dream: ay, there's the rub.*' Shakespeare's Hamlet, 1602

CHAPTER 22
THE SILENT PRAYER

Daily Philosophy

Life can be hard. Life can be so cruel. Yet, life is beautiful in all its excerpts. The silent screams of many are loud in their ears. Some will say, 'I will survive only if I tried harder. There would be no room for regrets for my mistakes. I have no control of the storms that come with each season. Yesterday is gone. If I tried today, it could get better tomorrow.'

Newton's Law of Motion emphasized…

"Change is the only constant thing in life…"

As long as we are blessed with this gift of life, it will take different turns to get us where we belong. Being strong is our only option in this puzzle called life.

There is no other choice, but to be strong. Life lessons 101.

We say a silent prayer now and then. We hide in our smiles, and even in our jokes. Sometimes, we live our lives in persona shifts, hoping that others would see us other than that which we really are. We dwell in pretenses while dying in silence.

One of the worst self-destructing behaviors is bottled emotions; it is death slow in coming. It is only natural to cry when your heart is heavy. It is very important and natural to always remember God. But, the way it is with most people, they remember God more when they are in need of His help.

Many people dream of coming to America with the hope of making better lives for themselves and for their families. Some Americans, with all the enviable rights and privileges accorded to them, are still ignorant of the fact they are blessed to have been born in the States; the world's greatest country. Those people not fortunate to have been born in America, not all, would love to trade places with any American, at least for a day.

Many Africans have died in the process of trying to become permanent U.S residents. The struggle to make one's life better remains the driving force behind most endeavors.

Walk with me to the end that marked the beginning of God's work in a silent prayer. In this short story, it was the silent prayer of a child. A prayer constantly said by a fourteen year old **Chidumebi (God lives with me)** *aka* **Dumebi**. He had just received a letter from the United States INS (Immigration and Naturalization Services) Office stating that he had won the Diversity Visa Lottery. It was Christmas in July for him, a dream come true for every one in his family. Dumebi sponsored his relocation to the United States by doing odd jobs. His mother was happy and sang songs of praise for everyone to hear. For a while, she was sad, knowing that her son would soon leave her. She knew she would be alone and somehow dreaded the moment even before it came.

Dumebi was a product of rape. In most African countries, it is an abomination to have a child out of wedlock. For this reason, her family disowned Dumebi's mother. She had nowhere else to run to, but to her church for support. She found refuge there. Dumebi was her life. Her experience as a rape victim was a burden she would carry with her for a long time.

She knew she would eventually allow her son to be independent. She had raised him teaching him all the right things, and had made sure his childhood and young adult orientations were pleasant experiences. At fourteen, Dumebi turned out to be an example of how every teenage boy ought to be.

The time for Dumebi to leave his home and travel to the United States came. Just before he left, he held hands with his overly emotional mother, and together they submitted all their petitions to God. Amazingly, both mother and son said the exact same silent prayer without knowing they had. All his mother could do was cry as Dumebi arrived at the airport security gate. With Dumebi, tears had formed in his eyes. He had no shame crying for his mother. She didn't leave after her son had boarded the airplane. She stood there beyond the fences, to watch the plane in its climb into the skies. He was gone. She was now all alone.

America is populated by people of all races. Dumebi was intimidated by the one common factor experienced by many before him; an accent. An accent makes each of us unique. However, he was very excited to be in the great United States. He was young, so it was easier for him to imbibe the American culture quite easily. And he did that in a short period of time. He communicated with his mother occasionally.

Shortly after his relocation, the aunt he was living with died. Dumebi was still under eighteen years old, and therefore was not considered of legal age. The State took possession of him and placed him in foster care. He did not understand what it meant to be a foster child in a foster home, with many other teenagers. Again, he said a silent prayer to ameliorate what he saw could become a harsh surrounding.

Foster homes are like playing the lotto. Only the lucky ones draw the lucky numbers. Life in a foster home is not determined by cracking a fortune cookie. Good foster homes happen by chance, and not by choice. Dumebi's path to his life's destination was altered when he became one of the teens in a foster home; another way one could get lost in America. At this point, he lost all communication with his mother. Life became a living hell for Dumebi. His mother was also living in misery, not sure what had happened to her only son. Just like her son, she did what she knew best; her silent entreaties to God were endless and persistent.

Dumebi became one of the many young adults who got lost in the American system of foster care. He lived here with six other teenage boys. Sibling rivalry was alive in full play. It was a volcano waiting to erupt. In every bad situation, Dumebi could only do one thing; he prayed silently. His foster brothers decided to nick-name him the 'Dummy' because he was not noisy, rude, indecent, callous, mischievous, arrogant, greedy, and was a lot more intelligent than they were. Dumebi was young, but had the wisdom of a sage. Eventually, he understood the system.

He knew his only way out was to reach the legal age of eighteen. He had less than four years to wait for his freedom. He focused on getting an education and eventually a job, so he'd be able to take care of himself and his mother back home in Nigeria. While he planned on his future, the devil was working hard to derail all of that. Good things come with obstacles. Well, not always. It takes the grace of God and total submission to Him to overcome the bottom-feeder; the devil.

At seventeen, Dumebi gained admission into the State University. His foster mother was so proud of him, while his foster brothers were obviously consumed with jealousy over his successes. His foster brothers' efforts leaned towards illegal drug business and consumption. The life of a drug addict is the life of illusion.

Dumebi had just finished saying his night prayers when he heard the sirens in the distance. He got up and looked out the window. Dumebi saw lights flashing; Police cars, three of them were in their driveway. Then, he heard the knock. The cops had come to his house. "Open up, Police," someone barked out the order. His foster mother opened the front door. And then, Dumebi was arrested for the murder of one his foster brothers. His brother was shot in the head outside of a club. Dumebi's photo identification card was found at the crime scene with blood stains. Dumebi had no alibi, but he had God on his side. He had not shot nor murdered anyone. He was nowhere near the crime scene, but he could not prove his innocence. Pretty soon, he was indicted for the crime. The case went to court. He was found guilty of murder and was sentenced to life in prison without the possibility of parole.

The path to his destiny suddenly took a turn for the worse. Only this time, it seemed like a dead-end. He cried and pleaded his innocence. But, it was his word against his foster brothers'. They accused him of an act they knew he had no part in. Dumebi was taken to prison. He had just turned eighteen years of age.

In the meantime, his mother in Nigeria became ill. Doctors were unable to determine why she was sick. She had been disconnected from her son for years; seven years to be precise. People told her that he must be dead since he had not contacted her all this time. In her heart, she knew otherwise. While she was in the hospital, a specialist doctor who was visiting from the United States to handle a very delicate medical case heard someone crying softly in one of the rooms. He knocked and went in. It was Dumebi's mother. When the doctor walked in, she quickly wiped away her tears and suppressed her emotions, but only for a moment. He asked, "Ma'am, are you okay?"

But her cries never waned. She needed a shoulder to cry on. She had cried all these years alone. The doctor sat next to her hospital bed. She asked him to pray with her. He obliged without any question. She said a silent prayer while the doctor quietly and gently held her hands. While she was silently praying, he looked at her. *She is very beautiful*, he thought to himself. Nevertheless, he prayed for her, asking God to *take away whatever pain this young woman was experiencing.*

After the tears and the praying had subsided, the doctor introduced himself. His name was **Chiagọziem (God has blessed me)** *aka* **Gọziem**. He also asked her if there was a way for him to help her, medically. She told him that she was fine and thanked him for praying with her. He wasn't sure how, but he wanted to know more about her.

Goziem found the courage and went back to visit her two days after. But, she had been discharged the day before. He was one unhappy doctor.

He wished he had listened to what his heart had mused upon…that first day.

Dumebi turned 21 in prison. He continued his education while incarcerated. His passion was to become a medical doctor. But he ended up studying law. He chose the legal profession so he could fight the swelling injustices in the system. For Dumebi, life had been rough, and now, he was paying for a crime he did not commit. He was paying for a crime he did not commit. On the day he turned 25, his case was reopened. There was an eye witness! This material witness had seen the actual triggerman that had fired the bullets that killed the victim. It was not Dumebi.

A fifteen year old boy at the time recorded the incident using his Nintendo DSi (with a video camera) while on his bike. He was afraid that if he had ratted on those boys, something bad would and could have happened to him. The boy on a bike, Anthony, was now 22 years old. He imagined himself in Dumebi's position and felt terrible for holding on to the secret that should have freed the innocent man. Anthony told his father about the burden he had been carrying. His father was a medical doctor with a law background. He was the same doctor that had visited Dumebi's mother in the hospital. Was this a twist of fate or what?

Dr. Gọziem decided he would personally handle the case. Dumebi's case was officially reopened. After a few months, the tables were turned, and Dumebi's foster brothers were arrested, indicted and sentenced for the crime Dumebi was accused of.

Dumebi had a few months left to graduate, before he would attend law school. Upon his release, the State paid him handsomely for false incarceration. He became friends with Dr. Gọziem and his family. He needed to do the one thing that he had yearned to do for so many years. He took a trip to Nigeria to visit his mother.

Dumebi's mother had moved from the home she raised her son in. The young man had lost all contact with his mother over the years. He took a trip to Abuja in search of her. It was a difficult task, but one that was worth the try.

After weeks of frustrated search, in an almost unfamiliar city, Dumebi had another conversation with God. While he prayed, his mother, 37 years old at this time, was rushing to catch a cab to go back home from the market. She felt a sudden urge to stop. So, she did. She stopped a few feet away from the spot where her son was standing, whispering the silent prayer.

He looked up momentarily, not sure why the woman standing three arms-lengths away from him had caught his attention. The woman had seen him first, and had stood rock-steady by the roadside staring at him. Their eyes met, and both were hit with flashbacks. Dumebi moved first, walking slowly toward her. He quickened his pace as the woman's feet gave way. She began to fall, and just as she was about to hit the tarmac, he grabbed her, and pulled her up. They stared into each other's face. And then, she muttered; "My God…could it be?" The crying began.

They sat on the roadside. She was exhausted, out of breath, in a reverie. When she snapped out of it, it was her lost son's face she was staring into. She rose, taking her time to do so, speechless and still in awe. She grabbed hold of his hand and began to massage it gently. Somewhere in her mind, she was waiting to wake from a second long-drawn-out dream. Not so! These drifts of small motions were causing her head to roll one side, and then the other. And the soft brown eyes staring back at her were familiar studs that once belonged to her five-year old. He was twenty-five years old now. And she could still smell her son; the scent that bound them was in the air, only stronger. Tears flowed, copiously. The embrace tightened, and for as long as it lasted, the world was vacant of people, and had stood still.

Who knew this moment would come? God did. Prayers were said, in silence. Hope once lost was regained, and at the destined time. Dumebi was reunited with his mother, **Chikọdili (It is up to God)**.

It was another Christmas in July for Dumebi and his mother. It was time to take care of his mother. So, he filed all the necessary documents with INS. Chikọdili relocated to the States with her son. They had so much to talk about. They both had their whole lives to share with each other, about the paths that led to this moment.

Back in the United States, Dumebi wanted his mother to meet his second family in America; Dr. Gọziem and his son. It was another day to be remembered.

Dumebi's mother had lived through some bad times. Emotionally, she was sapped, and her beauty could have receded somewhat. The 'depression'she lived with for a while hadn't affected her in any way. After she was reunited with her son, her recovery began and the new life that came with it was filled with promises. She was aglow, basking in memorable possibilities; the love from a man she had every reason to fall in love with was one. Well, the other; her son and the unification of a lifetime.

True happiness comes from within. She was a very beautiful woman. Again, God had a plan. Dr. Gọziem and his son, Anthony, honored Dumebi's invitation to meet his mother.

It is really amazing how God moves the puzzle pieces around to get us where we need to be. In the event that there are obstacles, it takes some time to reach the destination. But eventually, at God's appointed time, we'll get there.

Chikọdili convinced her son she would prepare a home cooked meal rather than dine in a fancy restaurant. As Dr. Gọziem and his son walked into Dumebi's apartment, his heart skipped a beat because his eyes saw what his heart had yearned for. He never thought he would see Chikọdili ever again; the lovable stranger. He was choked with emotion. *He looked familiar*, Chikọdili thought.

"Doctor, the woman in the blue dress is my mother," Dumebi said.

Dr. Gọziem froze up. When he thawed, his eyes popped open. With Chikọdili, she was lost in a time warp, wondering why this man was staring at her with eyes larger than your everyday demitasse spoon.

"I was the doctor that visited you while you were in the hospital in Abuja." Dr. Gọziem said. "Remember?" He asked.

"Oh yes, you are! Wait a second…" Chikọdili stumbled.

The doctor came to her aid. He closed the gap between them and took her in a bear hug. She wrapped her hands around him, holding him as tight as she could.

"It is you, Dr. Gọziem."

"Yes my dear, and in the flesh too!"

Dr. Gọziem's stomach was already filled with joy. Whether he could eat the food before him was in doubt. His heart was quietly doing a sommersault. He was hoping that this time he would summon the courage to ask for her hand in… Well, you guessed it.

Everyone was satisfied with the meal especially Dr. Gọziem.

Of course, they got married, eventually. At the celebration of their first wedding anniversary and thanksgiving, it was testimonial time! Chikọdili had so much to thank God for, as did her son.

Every step in life leads to somewhere. God is the reason that we are, and why we have hope in life. Imagine what your life would have been if God was not a part of it. He fights for the innocent. One thing is certain; God is never late, and His timing is always perfect.

All we need are simple conversations with God. There are no special times to say a silent prayer. Silent prayers can be said anytime, any day, and anywhere. God sees and knows our hearts at all times. He hears our every supplication; silent or spoken. It is really up to God to be gracious. He lives within each and every one of us.

CHAPTER 23

AN ANGRY HEART: A RAGING STORM

Like a storm, the heart of an angry man rages at the speed of light and sometimes, the outcome is irreversible.

Majority of Igbo women were murdered by those who were supposed to protect them; their husbands. It is happening with more frequency; the death of a woman in the hands of her husband. In some parts of Africa, men have used their wives for ritualistic acts (to gain wealth, political status, or hope to live for eternity). In the United States, from 2001 to present, approximately more than forty Igbo women have been brutally murdered by their husbands. The question remains: Why are some Nigerian husbands in the United States killing their wives?

Age can be a big factor in a marriage. Maturity is another. The struggle for power; the control of the couple's finances has always been a dueling issue. You would think infidelity should be a big part in divorces in many of these marriages. Not so! But, it carries its own weight when determining why couples fall the hard way. Today, a good number of persons in marriages merely exist, because it is the convenient thing to do. The couples are living miserably having to face each other everyday. They coexist for reasons, in some cases, neither of the couple could explain.

But they keep hoping.

Being hopelessly devoted has put many lives at risk. Indeed, it is a sad commentary about the grace of matrimony. What would drive one spouse into taking the life of the other? As it is in most cases, the wife, the same woman he had taken a vow to protect and '*...to love for better or worse, 'til death do them part'* becomes the victim.

There is an ongoing debate on the issue among young adults in African communities on why wives are being killed by their spouses. An African man gave this reason;

*"You African women come to America and buy into the American culture. You forget that back home, husbands are lords of the Jungle. Do not our mothers call our fathers, "**Nna anyi**?" Here, you turn your husbands into frustrated men and eventually, into murderers. Let's leave* ***dis oyibo*** *(Whiteman) way, and learn to live as Nigerian couples do back home. This is bitter truth!"*

Interesting!

A woman listening to the opinion that had come from a bona fide male chauvinist had a different take.

"It takes two to do the tango. However you choose to paint it, I want you to hear this; our men tend to be abusive to their spouses. The culture we come from has condoned it for years. If we, Igbo women ascribe to American culture, it does not give a man, regardless of cause, the right to take a life."

Here in America, when a man physically abuses his wife, and she reports it, the man would most likely be arrested and jailed. In most cases, the State would resort to the filing of charges, even if the abused woman wanted to recant her testimony.

Many African women would stay in a hopelessly known situation; she would take further abuses, including those that are mentally tasking. Well, tradition expects her to be devoted to her husband!

But wait…

"A nagging wife is like cancer in the bone." Proverbs 12:4.

It takes a man with the fear of God to seek His Grace when he is married to a 'nagging wife.'

Nagging is the big bad wolf. And when it comes from a woman, it is much more difficult to contain. This is the bane of most African marriages. Africans by nature are loud talkers. They are hyperbolic; they holler even when fun is in the mix. The sight of two African males in a verbal brawl is usually mindboggling and ear shattering. That is what the situation is at home with feuding couples. Neighbors have been known to call those in law enforcement to settle quarrels between African couples.

Some of these feuds begin with a wife who couldn't stop badgering her husband with sharp-edged words she is spewing at a hundred miles an hour. If she is unlucky and draws a husband who is equally sharp-tongued, the fight usually is taken to a level both man and wife couldn't escape from.

Take the case of **Ndụbụisi (Life is Key)**. In a heartbeat, he had snapped. And without thinking anything about the consequences of his intended action, he went ahead and killed his wife. His four children suddenly had no parent in the home. After the murder, he was arrested and sentenced to life in prison. Ndụbụisi was not remorseful for his action. In his mind, he was justified for killing her. "She pushed me so hard, I snapped," he had told the Judge.

Ndụbụisi married his wife, **Nkechinyere (The one God has given)** *aka* **NkeChi,** in Nigeria before bringing her to the United States. Their traditional marriage and church wedding lasted for three days, with a large number from both families coming from overseas. Their marriage at the onset was full of hope. But, things began to go sour after the first two years. You'd think their disagreements would roll with time and then level out. It didn't in this case. Each fight was bigger than the last one. Eventually, it all exploded.

NkeChi had gone through the rigors of nursing school. It was what her husband wanted. No harm there. But, she would have prefered to be a Physical Therapist (PT). Well, her husband had spoken, and the choice was no longer hers. So, she hurriedly dropped the idea to become a PT to please her husband. In short, she submitted to his every whim. He made no sacrifices himself, but pushed her even further. NkeChi decided that she would not be just an RN (Registered Nurse). In a few years, she got her Master's in Nursing. She didn't stop there; with time, she became a Certified Professional in Healthcare Quality (CPHQ).

Ndụbụisi was very excited only because it meant more income for him. He then quit his job, became the proverbial lounge lizard. He did no small tasks, like getting the children ready for school. It was beneath him. As a consequence, his children were always late, especially in getting to the bus stop on time. Other tasks suffered as a consequence. NkeChi would leave work to keep the doctor's appointment with her children. She got no help from Ndụbụisi.

It was obvious NkeChi was the bread winner. Each payday, she was expected to hand over her paycheck to him. The hardworking woman went beyond the call of matrimony to please this dye-in-the-wool misogynist. It wasn't his paycheck, but it was always his decision on how the money was spent. He was in total control indeed; the captain of this ship. NkeChi was brilliant and ambitious, but not astute enough to listen to her heart. He was the quintessential bully. He made her miserable, until the day the end came for her.

Most nurses in the United States work twelve-hour shifts. Many bury themselves in their work to run away from marital chaos. NkeChi worked overtime just to have some extra money to care for herself, her children and her extended family. She barely had time for herself. When she got home, she was exhausted. But not once was it noted that she neglected to take care of her children, and yes, the bully.

Just like most battered women, NkeChi was hopeful that her situation would change for the better. Even as the situation got worse, her belief in her marriage never waned. The words that came out of Ndụbụisi's mouth were toxic. He talked down on his wife; telling her she was ugly, and that no man would be attracted to her, at least not after she had had four children. The hidden fact was that Ndụbụisi felt inadequate because of her earning power. Frustration mounted over time.

Ndụbụisi had unlimited time in his hands. He knew how he could make things go up against her. So, he came up with another plan. He called his friends, accusing his wife of infidelity.

She was a strong woman… this NkeChi. Inspite of the abuses, she proffered a persona to hide the pain she was feeling. She wasn't just strong; she had the fear of God in her.

Her family begged her to leave him. They had forgotten that she wanted her marriage to work more than anything in the world. Her reply to those kinds of suggestions was always terse: *I don't want to be a single mother. I want my kids raised in a home with both parents.*

NkeChi stayed. She endured, hoping that peace would find her. In one of their heated arguments, the night before Christmas, Ndụbụisi loudly told his wife; *'I will kill you very soon, if your behavior doesn't change. You cannot withdraw money from our joint account without my permission.'*

For the first time, she talked back, yelling almost. *'Go to hell,'* she said to him. That night could have been the day his hatred for her took a turn for the worse. It was also on this night that she nursed the idea of leaving his sorry *ass*. She decided she would wait for the right opportunity to move out of the house with her childen.

The day she was bludgeoned to death was her day off.

She did her usual chores; cleaned, cooked, laundered, and then decided to take a short nap before the children got back from school. Her husband waited like the predator that he was. Finally, NkeChi drifted off.

He would sniff the air in the house; his tongue had thrust out like a serpent tasting the wind to find its prey. He found the bedroom she was in; one of the children's room. His time had come, and as with all beasts of prey, he had begun to salivate like a Komodo dragon.

She was laying in her son's room, unaware of what was about to happen to her. Ndụbụisi knew how tired she was. He walked like a cat on the prowl and pushed the door open. He stood there, watching her, seeing how peaceful she looked in her sleep. He got madder. Even the small, almost inaudible snore NkeChi was making had begun to annoy him. Then, he smiled to himself, a sinister kind of smile. Moments later, he moved away from the door to fetch a blunt instrument.

He grabbed a metal object he had hidden in his trunk and returned to the room where his wife was sleeping. The sudden rush of adrenaline blinded him momentarily. To clear his vision, he shut his eye tight to bring back his sanity, and ascertain he was in control. He mouthed this phrase; "Just one hit will do it."

The first hit was mushed; the instrument ricocheted off his hands. He grabbed it, and slowly raised it above his head, now that his prey was incapacitated. Still, he continued hitting her. Ten blows to the head. He knew she was dead, but he just couldn't stop himself.

The room was covered with blood. His hands and face dripped blood. In a flash, he thought of his children. That thought stopped him, however briefly. But the man was on a roll. Five more hits later, he finally stopped, breathing like a marathon runner. His eyes caught the haunting scene he had created; the bloody canvas sprinkled with brain matter. He grabbed some sheets from the next room and covered her up. All of a sudden, the murderer was feeling hunger pangs. Ndụbụisi left the bloody room and returned to the kitchen for the *fufu* she had prepard for him before going for the nap.

Ndụbụisi forgot the meaning of his name. He could have made another choice that would have prevented this regrettable deed. He could have filed for divorce. He could have gone back to work, if he had looked. He could have prayed, and asked God for help. He could have taken a deep breath to calm his soul. He could have done a lot of things to end his marriage if he wanted to. Rather, he chose to kill her.

What got him was the kind of time he had in his hands to plot evil. *An idle man is indeed in a devil's workshop.* Ndụbụisi was a deranged man and didn't know it. After he had constructed it, there was no going back; his mind couldn't rewrite the tracjectory of his evil musings. It resulted in the killing of his wife, the mother of his four children, the woman he had lived with for many years!!!

How could any woman (or any man) absorb so much abuse and still remain in the marriage? How could a woman not tell that her relationship was in shambles, and could not be repaired? Why would any woman lie to herself about the dangers she faces daily, looking into the eyes of her could-be killer and not know it?

If you are a woman, you should ask yourself this question: Do I need this marriage to make me whole; to complete me?

CHAPTER 24

PEEK-A-BOO… WHEN THINGS FALL APART

There are too many reasons why things fall apart in our lives and in our relationships. Most friendships are founded on a wake of cards; the foundation hardens with time, or collapses on the ever shifting block it was erected on. There are a host of things that would determine the longevity of every relationship. They include communication, or lack thereof. The list is a mile long, and each has the potential to erase long-standing relationships, or as a consequence of it, make it stronger.

In the midst of all that goes on in our lives, baring insanity, we are very aware of the choices we make. Our lives are strengthened, emboldened or, we are damned to exist poorly and below expectations from the choices we make. With every wrong decision, things begin to fall apart before our eyes.

ỌnyekaChi (Who is greater than God?) *aka* **KaChi** was the sixth of seven children. Raised in a healthy environment; her childhood orientation was a very happy one. Her father and mother were the quintessential couple; they loved each other dearly. KaChi saw that, and of course, learned from it. She looked up to her parents, and hoped she would have the kind of love her parents had to share with whomever she would eventually share her life with. Her parents had shielded her as a teenager. Even as she reached adulthood, they never quite left her on her own. KaChi was guarded wholesomely, and was provided for. The truth of the matter was that she lacked nothing.

It wasn't just material things that she got; she was spiritually enriched. Her parents made sure they instilled the fear of God in her. The virtue of celibacy, she also understood, to the point where she knew that her body was a temple of God, and must not be defiled before marriage. She was indeed a virgin until she met, courted, and married the boy next door, Stanley.

Sadly, with her marriage to Stanley, she had walked into a beehive. She knew that after the first month had passed, and the touches and whispers had died down, replaced by shouts and steely stares from Stanley. In her mind, it was too early for any kind of fight between them. So, KaChi would do more to sweeten and freshen up the space she shared with her husband. That meant, she cooked more, became more sensual as a way of keeping him satisfied on all fronts. Her good-naturedness was in overdrive, even as she got nothing in return.

KaChi had been dealt a terrible hand. Nothing she did worked. Her tactics appeared to be blowing up in her face, threatening her marriage. The house she and Stanley lived in was always abuzz with his invented shenanigans and made-up stories to ignite a fight. Whether he would win the war was another thing. KaChi wasn't showing any signs that she had had enough. She was rolling with his punches; turning the other cheek, and hoping he would wake up one day and just cease.

But the man never waned in his style of abuse; he would employ other tactics, meaner than the ones he had used in the past. KaChi was emotionally and psychologically drained. As a consequence, Stanley was enjoying his mastery over her, knowing that his wife had nowhere to run to. "She would stay in the marriage even if it killed her, virtuous woman,' he once mused on the curious situation he knew his wife was in.

KaChi believed her marriage would work because they had known each other since they were in kindergarten. She talked to herself more… wondering what it was she was doing wrong. *It's not Stanley's fault. It is my fault.* It was the wish of her parents' that had manifested in her relationship with Stanley. She was incapable of extricating herself from any kind of blame, and as a consequence, had suffered immeasurably from it.

The secrets to a happy marriage are there for the taking. But, what works for Jack and Jill may or may not work for the couple next door. Marriage does not come with a manual on how tos. Understanding the basic tenets of life and love are the guiding forces behind any successful marriage. We must learn as we go; learn from our mistakes to be wiser. These are some of the facts of life, and KaChi's mother had probably instilled those in her too. She could also have learned from her mother how to be a good wife. Whether that had helped her is anybody's guess. Her father, in his time, could have told her about the role a man plays in his household. Maybe it was that infallible nature of man, in this case, her husband's that caused her to withstand his abuses for as long as she was able to.

Two years after their wedding, they were still living happily. If that were to be the measure by which all marriages were gauged, then her marriage to Stanley should have been a success. Yes, Stanley was not romantic. KaChi accepted his dull romantic style as part of the package. Even before the honeymoon was over, he had turned insensitive to her needs. One wonders why she had stayed. And in the painful realities confronting her daily, she became pregnant. Now, she would have nowhere to go, she thought. This side of his personality, KaChi did not see while courting Stanley for eight months.

The physical intimacy stopped immediately when she got pregnant. Stanley was barely at home. Most times when a woman gets pregnant, her hormones take over. For the next forty weeks, nature was busy rewriting portions of who she really was. And when she drew from the bushel, and proffered a hand thereafter, it was usually weird in its passage; there were tell-tale signs that her mind could be flying at half mast. Understandably, overnight, she had grown overly gregarious. It is a crap shoot, a roll of the dice. Whatever number that came up demanded that her husband fill the blanks and granted her what she wanted from that page, good or bad. These were the newer parts of her that were rarely seen or noticed. It would therefore take an attentive, caring, and sensitive husband to accommodate, the sometimes weird demands his wife made. A pregnant woman needs tender loving care. And who is there to provide those for her? Her husband…that's who!

But, as was the case with KaChi, the man she married was flagrantly missing from her life, even as they lived together under one roof. KaChi lacked everything, including all that could have made her pregnancy a lot easier for her. For a husband who was never around, she had no other choice, but to go it alone.

Many married couples are lonely and single, even as they are snared in the existence of each other's company. There are early signs when things start to go bad with the threat of totally falling apart. The issues causing the rift between couples must be fixed early to prevent irreparable damage. But, many ignore the blatant signs for obvious reasons.

Nine months later, KaChi had the baby, a girl. She named her **Kasiemobi (Heal/restore my heart)** *aka* **Kasie.** Months after the baby was born, and KaChi had recovered from the rigors of being pregnant, she began to express her concerns and fears to her husband. She came up with some ideas to sweeten their marriage, suggesting that they rekindle their love for each other, by going out on dates and going away for the weekend. She even picked vacation spots in far exotic locales to light this fire. She cooked often, cleaned and cared for him with the same affection as she applied to her newborn. She was a beautiful woman at heart, and nothing her husband did would dampen her spirit.

Stanley only acknowledged her on the moments his libido surged. She succumbed to his yearnings because she was the submissive wife. Stanley had it his way, and he was happy for that.

Truth is indeed a stranger where evil lurks. One does not have to be a murderer to be evil. It is evil when you knowingly hurt and defile another person by your words and/or by your actions. Stanley refused to mend his ways, even as he stared goodness in the face every morning when he woke up.

He provided for the family grudgingly. The presence of his newborn served to corral his wild thoughts, especially those that bothered on physical abuse of KaChi. For as long he was able to provide for them, he believed his job was done, and no woman under his care should even try to tame his vituperations.

The Igbos also believe that when a man impregnates his wife, the burden of pregnancy should not fall on the woman alone. Getting a woman pregnant seems to be the easy part. It takes a real man to do the right thing and love his wife, especially when she is with child. Stanley had this notion backwards. He was one of those men that believed that women should be indebted to men. In other words, for a man to single out a woman and marry her, she should owe him immeasurable gratitude and eternal servitude, even if she finds herself in the midst of so much pain and anguish.

Sadly, there are many Stanleys out in the world.

For KaChi, she did her best to live with the nightmare she was married to. She remained in the marriage, and as a result, she became pregnant with her second baby. The inhumane treatments continued. This second pregnancy didn't go the way the first one did. She had complications; one in which the placenta grows in the lowest part of the womb (uterus) and covers all or parts of the opening to the cervix. The condition caused heavy bleeding, thus making her situation high risk. Her doctor advised her to be on bed rest and abstain from sexual intercourse. This could have stirred Stanley's mind to ebb and flow in every imaginable dark recess. He still chose to have intercourse with the wife he despised. It was not clear if he did so to castigate, in his own way, the doctor's order he felt was an affront to his person and his household. And during the said intercourse with his wife, he was neither gentle; he took it forcefully, snaring at her like a hyena fighting off another animal for a meal. Her condition at the time meant nothing to him.

Stanley repeatedly raped his 'high risk' pregnant wife until she started bleeding profusely. Guess who got scared? Yes, Stanley! He called for help. KaChi was rushed to the hospital.

As luck would have it, she survived the trauma, but did not carry the baby to term. The baby weighed four pounds and seven ounces. Again, she had a name for her son before he was born. She called him **Onyemaechi (Who knows tomorrow?)** *aka* **Onyema**.

With a baby boy born to Stanley, his mood swings abated somewhat. It looked as if having a boy was the reason he changed course with his behavior and feelings toward mother and child. KaChi took all that in stride, hoping it wasn't going to be short-lived. She urged him to get help if he wanted their marriage to work. *'If not for me, do it for the children, Stanley...'*

Amazingly, he told her that she too needed help. It became clear why he had taken some time off to rein in his bad behavior; he hadn't done so for his wife. It was the joy of having a son born to him that put him in a happy mood. But, it was all short-lived; his evil ways returned. The birth of his son had done nothing to steer him from being a bad husband.

The only way KaChi could keep her sanity going was to pray through songs on a daily basis. Since she had no one to talk to, besides engaging in little banter of baby-talk with her little ones, she spoke to God through songs.

One of the songs was by Maranatha Singers; 'I will be with you' played in her head. She gave it voice; singing it out loud, and crying every time the same song rolled in her head.

"God be with me, in joy and in pain, my cry for mercy echoes your name. Now and forever..., God be with me. My prayer for deliverance will not be denied. Fight my battle..."

A straight from the heart prayer through song!

One morning as she sang one of her songs, crying uncontrollably, tears gushing, her body shaking from severe spasms, her husband stood at a distance watching what he believed was an act. She was in the baby's room, cuddling the little infant in her arms, rocking him back and forth while singing. Stanley heard bits and pieces of the song, and immediately drew a tortured conclusion; that the song was all about him. That she was deliberately rebuking him in the most feared of ways: The call to God for hurried vengeance. Stanley ran into the nursery room, snatched the baby from her and laid him down in his cot. Next, he grabbed his wife, who at this moment, had yet to figure out what was happening. Until the beating began, her brain was slow in alerting her of the danger she was facing.

Battered like a crushed watermelon, she was laying on the nursery room floor, moaning for help.

Like always, she recovered from the latest drubbing. Only this time, she stayed just a couple of days in the hospital. On the second and last day of her hospital stay, she had songs to lead and heal her broken spirit. Listening to her, you couldn't tell she was in the hospital and recovering from such a terrible beating.

The song went like this:

"I have a Great Jesus. He is the bright morning star. From ages to ages, you are God, from generation to generation, from January to December; I have a Great Jesus..."

As KaChi sang unabashedly, eyes shut, hands flailing, someone else was in the room with her, watching her sing, and greatly enjoying her talent. It was the same nurse that had been taking care of KaChi. She stood with rapt attention, leaning against the door, her own tears running, wondering how such a battered woman could find anything in her frail body to support such performance.

One week had passed since KaChi returned home. Half of her face was still wired with several stitches. Her wrecked emotional state had not left her. But one thing was certain; the beating had left her a much stronger woman, and she was determined to move on with her life… without her husband. This was true, because her faith in God had strengthened.

But first, Stanley must be held accountable for the beatings she had received. Charges were filed. Stanley was arrested and placed in the county jail. While he was cooling his heels, awaiting trial, KaChi had enough time to pack up and leave the house.

KaChi's heart was completely broken, but not her spirit. She endured both emotional and physical traumas. She drew strength from her weakness, and then took her pain and turned it into power. She refused to dwell on the beatings that had nearly killed her. But the trauma of being nearly deformed and paralysed from his constant physical abuses was a hard thing to shed. After she had fully recovered, her mind was telling her to go back to school. So she did. She went back to school to complete her dissertation for her doctorate in Psychology.

What better way to fully understand a situation than when you have been in it, she thought to herself. She devoted her life to being happy, raising her two children and counseling women in situations like the one she had experienced. (**Who is indeed greater than God? (OnyekaChi)**, **Console my heart (Kasiemobi)**, and **Who knows tomorrow? (Onyemaechi)**).

No one obviously knows tomorrow, but God.

KaChi lived her life one day at a time, with the hope of finding the kind of love God had in store for her. It didn't take long, and neither was it late for her.

When things fall apart, destinies are changed, hearts are broken, homes are wrecked, and lives are shattered too, sometimes lost. But, for the strong, not all hope is lost.

CHAPTER 25
BEHIND THE CLOUDS

The beauty of the ocean is not just the serenity of the waves, or the shimmering colors formed over it. It is the swarming, screaming life beneath its surface that constitutes the nearly beatific grandeur that holds us in awe. It is more than we can ever imagine. Have you ever considered the depth of the ocean; what goes on in the mysterious pit? The ocean's secrets run deep just like the heart of a woman. Naturally, women are molded to endure even the highest level of pain: Childbirth. They are fashioned to submit to the laws of nature and not to that particular law of man: Cruelty!

Some men say a woman is like a rose; tend to it with soft touches, and it will blossom. Other men would liken a woman to food; women are there to be sampled as in taste-testing. The lucky morsel of womanhood would be placed in a Gordiva candy wrap and taken home. Her duties would include making sure her husband's sexual hunger was quenched. Just as the saying goes: *Keep his stomach full and his balls empty.* The woman becomes her husband's favorite meal, until the erstwhile vibrant taste in his mouth begins to turn stale. At this time, most men would start looking for fresh juices to resurrect their dormant pallets. In other words, a new woman, with bold mixture of sweetness and wildness would do to stir him. That wife at home, the same one of noble character would be placed inadvertently, to play second fiddle in a jazz trio. One of his reasons for staying cozy with another woman is that his wife *nags him all the time.* 'A nagging wife is like cancer in the bone.' The bible also says that "A wife of noble character is her husband's crown, but a disgraceful wife is like decay in his bones." Proverbs 12:4.

In a marriage, many African couples endure immeasurable amounts of emotional pain and degradation. Physical abuse is part of the package. In the eyes of many, it is dubbed 'sacrifice.' They strongly believe in that, while praying for a miracle. Here is the truth: Women who sacrifice their happiness and freedom to remain in clearly abusive marriages are not always lucky in their quest. Usually, their investment yields them no return. It is no surprise that one finds them wielding the short end of the stick, as in losing their lives, in some instances. There have been tales of the ever obedient and submissive wives, especially with the ones that would readily ignore the threat facing them.

It is amazing how one person's life is destroyed, and another's sorrow is turned into joy, by a simple twist of fate. This is a situation of two women: **KaneneChi (Let's look up to God)** *aka* **Kanii**, and **Udoka (Peace is greater)**.

This is their story…

Kanii found her true love and married him. His name was Joe. Joe came into the marriage with everything he had, as did Kanii. The script of their union was probably written in Heaven. Yes, it was that strong! But, with the seeming vastness in their love for each other, Joe's family never quite joined the feast. His mother and father couldn't hide their distaste for Kanii.

As is the case in most African culture, the woman is blamed for childlessness. Kanii would have to find a way to explain her fertility problem to the growing number of in-laws determined to send her away, and have Joe remarry. With Joe, he was never bothered by his family's distaste for his wife.

Childbearing is God's gift, and man couldn't affect it one way or the other. The pressures he was feeling to let his wife go strengthened him instead. He would hold hands with his wife in public as a way of admonishing the bitterness spewing from family members. It was clear that Joe and Kanii loved each other. Shortly after they renewed their vows like they did each year, Joe was carjacked. The car thieves took him to a remote part of town, and killed him. Just like that!

No surprises there… Kanii was blamed for the death of her husband. She was accused of hiring the assassins that killed him. The motive they surmised was that Kanii wanted to inherit his wealth.

Over our dead bodies, they moaned.

Her heart was broken. Nevertheless, she did her best to ignore her in-laws' accusations. She waited for the burial to pass, before she would mount her own defense. But in the interim, her life was filled with misery.

It didn't end there. Kanii was humiliated in the village square. She was told to drink the bath water used to wash her husband's corpse to prove her innocence. She refused. The accusations took a turn for the worse. She was castigated as if she was an outcast. Overnight, she had become a pariah. She pleaded to be left alone, swearing in God's name that she was innocent. But, it all fell on deaf ears.

Kanii had nowhere to run to. She had no one to turn to either. Her choice was clear; she would turn to her God to rescue her, as always. She began having conversations with The Father upstairs.

No one was sure how it had happened; who had dispensed the poisonous potion she had swallowed during an evening meal? Two days had passed, and the culprits in the village were waiting in the wings for Kanii to drop dead. *What were her conversations with her God that had kept her going?* Was Kanii aware she had been poisoned? It was rumored that the potion administered to her was large enough to slow down a herd of elephants. Why was she still standing and seemingly unbothered by the uncut cyanide they had fed her? The villagers were shocked and disappointed. They had failed. The plotters took another route. They had her arrested and then tied her to a tree trunk in a corner of the local shrine.

But God had other plans for Kanii.

On the second night of her capture and imprisonment, while the guards themselves were sleeping, the winds began to howl. A shadow fell among the trees, stepped up on the mound where she was and nudged Kanii from her sleep. She thought she was in a dream and could only stir her consciousness into a-not-so-thoughtful wakeful mode. But the squeaky sounds persisted, and could have been what had stirred the guards themselves. They heard the noise and rose with lethargy, and somehow managed to walk to where Kanii was tied up.

But the bizarre noise that had started next door had begun to appear distant. The guards found the frequency and without hesitation, drifted away from the area where Kanii was shackled against the tree. The coast was clear, and the tap on her shoulder was no longer implied; it was real as the roughness of the tree she was leaning against. Now, she was fully awake, staring into the dark emptiness, wondering what it was that had brushed against her. Kanii saw nothing, and felt nothing. But her skin cropping into small bumps disabled her further. Her mind prompted her to fight the looming silence for a moment of reality. *Oh God, just a minute of your time would do... this... this... Oh my God... please...!!!*

Then she heard the voice; the voice was foreign, cool, as in calming her rioting nerves down. *It's time to go.* She felt the warm wind pass over her with just an ounce of elegiac force. It could lull her back to sleep, but the whispering voice had blended with the wind, and Kanii was listening to the symphony it had become; the soothing melodies in rhapsody, the merging of fears and greater courage into a mixture of angelic ballads. The rope that held her tight against the tree had loosened. She discarded the rope and stood up in the dark. Not sure what was happening, she quietly walked away from it all. Kanii encountered none of the guards on her way out. They seemed to have disappeared. *What could have happened to them? Who untied me?* Kanii asked herself. As if someone was after her, she ran as fast as her legs could have carried her.

On the other side of the country, lived **Udoka** and her husband, **Edozie** (Short for **Chiedozie** meaning: **God has preset/done it**). Udoka had one thing in common with Kanii; they both had no children. The only difference was that Udoka got pregnant a few times, but lost it all. However, much bigger differences existed in their lives: While Kanii was faithful to her husband; it was not the case with Udoka who cheated on her husband every chance she got. While Edozie loved and cherished his wife, Udoka, Kanii suffered at the hands of her husband's kinfolks.

The story of Udoka and Edozie is a painful one, yet classic. How Edozie survived it couldn't be explained. But he did. In the face of flagrant, multiple betrayals on the part of his wife, you could tell the whole gist of a sordid tale, which no part of it would have made Edozie remain in the marriage.

Four miscarriages later, Udoka became pregnant with her fifth child. How happy could Edozie be? He was as happy as a child who just got a Christmas gift from Santa. He was grateful to God that Udoka could be impregnated again, given the scourges that followed her previous losses. But as his joy was mounting and rolling as would one on a roller coaster, he had no idea what was waiting for him at the next bend.

Seven weeks into the pregnancy, Udoka walked into the home she shared with her husband, and started crying. The tears were copious, making Edozie believe she had lost the baby again. He lowered himself on the living room floor, and without asking her the reason for her own tears, cried out in anguish. He knew without been told that she had lost the baby.

If only he knew!

It was what Udoka was hoping she would get out of her husband; the need for her to appear genuine and convincing in her own trip. As long as there were no signs that would expose her double life, or where she was coming from, then, she would have succeeded. Udoka took over, taking her husband in her arms and consoling him. "We will try again," she cooed.

Two hours later, with no tears left to shed, Edozie got up and carried his wife with him into the bedroom. They spent the night in each other's arms, consoling and nibbling on each emotion that surfaced 'til morning came. It was how he took care of all other situations that had reared its ugly face. Now, he had learned to live with the hand nature had dealt him. His love for his wife never wavered. It was consistent. Only his wife didn't learn from her mistakes, and couldn't feel any sympathy for her husband. In her mind, she was doing the right thing. *Until she knows that the child she is carrying is her husband's, all pregnancies must be aborted.*

She had no reason to stop seeing John Langley.

John Langley lived on the other side of the railroad tracks. The problem wasn't that her sexual appetite was insatiable, it was the fact that John Langley was dapper, and with enough cash to buy the Bellagio. As mean as she was with her ways, she never brought any of the money she earned turning tricks with the man from Saskatchewan, Canada.

Shortly after Udoka aborted her fifth child, she returned to work. Not too long after that, she was arranging another tryst with the man with the deep pockets. She had convinced Mr. Langley to visit her at home instead. *It would be an adventure of a lifetime, one that would live in my memory,* she told him.

Udoka left work early one day pretending to be a little under the weather. On her way home, she stopped at a corner store to pick up anything that would add punch to her scheme. She was looking for that something extra that would accelerate the libido of the tallest man out of Canada. Good golly, she was on a roll. Udoka purchased grounded aphrodisiac, the color of milkshake. She also bought an ounce of cudweed soaked in eighty-proof Kentucky Bourbon. Her man would then be enabled, and his appetite would surge and spillover. The encounter she had built up in her mind could cause the world to move. *Only he had asked her to move it.*

In her twisted mind, she wanted this particular enslavement concluded inside the same minute that her husband should be walking into their home.

When she got home, she built herself a warm bath, soaked in it for a while, as she dreamed of his hands on her. Those moments when her husband's hands took over, Udoka would throw her eyes wide open to arrest the contentment she believed she was losing. When she had conjured up the images of the most beautiful man she had ever seen, she would then shut her eyes, and sink lower into the tub to imagine the hands and warm breath of John Langley on her.

On this day, she had everything a crafty, cheating woman would have in her repertoire; lingerie, and an intoxicating perfume that would make her smell and feel like a real woman, and of course, set John Langley's body ablaze.

When she stepped out of the tub, her naked body glowed. She stood in front of the bathroom mirror, admiring her nudity, and wondering why goddesses like her should be made to wear any clothing. Her mind had constructed a song by her favorite artist. 'Stay' by Jodeci, rolled in her head. Udoka imagined a glass of wine in her hand, and the only reason one hadn't appeared in those hands was because she was living in a Magic Island. But, soon, Mr. Langley would make it so. She closed her eyes, let her mouth wide open while taking in deep breaths to slow down her runaway heart. When she recovered, she left the bathroom for her bedroom, found a glass, a half-full bottle of wine, and poured herself a good measure. She walked to her bed, slithering into it as would a snake.

Seconds later, John Langley walked into another man's bedroom, to live through what the devil himself, had underwritten. He loved what he saw. With time passing, the moment was filled with angst because his mistress' husband could walk in on them, and the dapper dan would be unable to walk the walk. He froze up, but starred down hard on the beauty spread out before him. His manhood had taken a beating, and soon began to show life. Anger rushed him. He hated himself, wondering why he was flaccid at the onset. He changed tactics and gently sat next to her. He kissed her here, and stroked her there, with his eyes fixated at the bedroom door.

However, she was on fire as she waited for her body to be devoured. John Langley sat bolt upright, left the bed and walked into the bathroom. He ran a cold shower and forced himself to go under the needle-like sharpness of the running water. He woke up from his lethargy, and from the fetters of could-be sudden death. His erection shot through the cascade of the streaming shower. A smile lit his face, and he began to coo: "Here I come, baby." The proud Canadian was his old self again. With manhood in his hand, he stepped out of the shower, walked into the bedroom with a swagger only a swashbuckler would love.

But their timing was off… way off.

Edozie walked in on them. Helter skelter! The cool Canadian mist turned into a block of frozen meat, unable to move. When he realized his life could be in danger, he finally ran for the window, naked like a Jay bird. No luck there. He threw his hands up. The erection that called up his bad boy nature seconds ago, shriveled, and the stump it had become could have disappeared entirely, now that he knew the dog owner was in the bedroom with them.

The mild-mannered Edozie was confused for a second. He could have lost his sanity at seeing his beloved wife in the arms of another man. The wave of short-lived emotions swelled in his head. He was having flashbacks, and the images he was getting were blinding him, causing the room he shared with these cheaters to swirl. Colors were added to the stomping his mind was receiving, and they came in three-dimensional montages. Each band of vista threatened to blow up his head. Edozie's hands grabbed his head to rein the scowls of tattered landscape his mind was constructing. *Breathe...* he muttered to himself. *Breath... breathe... anụ ọfia... breathe,*" he hissed at himself.

When the fog cleared, Edozie opened his eyes, and then realized he was alone in his own bedroom. It had been two hours since he saw his wife getting whacked by another man. Edozie had begun to doubt that he had seen what he thought he had seen. Could it be that his eyes were lying to him? He got up, left the bedroom for a walk around the house. He couldn't find his wife anywhere around. The doubt he had resurfaced: He had fainted, and had had a nightmare. He returned to his bedroom and tried to force himself to sleep. Edozie was succeeding, until his wife's voice broke the reverie he was already into.

"I have come to make my confession, and ask for your forgiveness..." she began.

Edozie rolled over. His wife looked like the spitting image of Elvira, the witch. "You deserve to know the truth, Edozie, only I do not know where to start."

"What are you talking about?" He asked, wiping the film of weariness from his eyes.

The look on Udoka's face was that of a confused woman. *Had he not seen me in a compromising position with another man?* She whispered.

"Edozie, I have been unfaithful to you."

So, it is true... what my eyes had seen. Edozie thought to himself.

"Well, I am glad you are telling me. At some point, I could've sworn it was a bad dream."

For the next half hour, Udoka spilled her guts and all of her dangerous *sexcapades* with John Langley. Nothing was held back, including the misfortune Edozie had felt thinking that his wife's various miscarriages were exactly that.

"No, I had each pregnancy aborted because I had no way of knowing who the real father was," she said.

Edozie wanted death that instant. His heart succumbed to so much hurt. He was paralyzed and unable to rise from the bed. He shut his eyes, and prayed for death to rescue him. This much anguish and pain would even take a longer time to kill him.

In an African community, most times when a marriage is annulled or broken, it is the woman that usually leaves the home instead of the man. But in this case, Edozie chose to leave the home he had built with the woman he thought was his life partner. He knew he could not live in the house with the despicable images floating about in his mind. His marriage was over.

Life must go on, regardless!

In Nigeria, especially among the Igbos, a marriage is not over until it is broken traditionally. The dowry (bride price) paid on the woman must be returned. Neither the woman nor the man can marry another until all traditional ties linking the man and woman together are severed.

Edozie was heartbroken, disgusted by his wife's behavior, and could not wait to sever all bonds with her, especially when children were not involved. So, he decided to go to his village and inform his family and the elders of his intentions to let his wife, Udoka, go.

POSTSCRIPT

The day that Edozie chose to travel to the village was the same day Kanii was rescued from the shackles that once held her prisoner. She was running from her captors, gunning for the open road ahead of her. A car was coming in the distance. Her mind hadn't registered that. Kanii scaled a mound, and found herself in the middle of the road. The speeding car screeched to a halt to avoid hitting her. Her eyes were rolling so fast. She appeared dazed. The only reaction she could muster from a confounded mind was to sit on the tarmac in front of the car. The person driving the car must know she was running for her life. It was her hope that help had arrived.

Edozie stepped out of his car. The woman cowered on the road had fear written all over her. His greater instinct told him that she had to be running for her life. He wondered what or who could be chasing her. He stood next to her, actually, leaning toward her as he looked her in the eyes. It was his way of assuring her that he was not going to harm her. Kanii was still rooted in mild fear and could not throw all her hopes on this stranger. The battering she had received at the hands of her captors flooded her mind. Naturally, she pulled back from Edozie.

"It's okay. I am not going to hurt you," he said to her.

It was the right thing to say to a beleaguered soul. Kanii then took his hand. He pulled her up gently, careful not to make any sudden moves. He led her to his car, his hand over her shoulder.

Kanii had some time to look her rescuer over, as he was driving. He didn't look threatening for sure. When she found her voice, she spoke, but chewed on every other word, before she spat them out. Edozie turned to stare at the woman he believed could have lost her will, surprised she was speaking to him with such clarity in her voice. Edozie wondered who she was running from. When she was done with the story of how she had been on the run for her life, Edozie decided he would have to take her to his village. His hometown should bring with it, a measure of safety and hopefully, cause the paralyzing fear she was feeling to disappear.

Two weeks later, Kanii was still staying with Edozie in his village. People had started to wonder if she was truly someone he had picked off the roadway. They wanted another version of the story told, something more believeable than the one most in the village were aware of and didn't think was true. Could it be that he had chosen this woman in lieu of the one he had married? Why was there nothing done to take the woman to her own hometown?

After two months of Kanii living with Edozie in his parents' home, the villagers had started to think that Kanii had found a permanent home. Edozie wasn't too far behind with his own reflections regarding the possibility that he had seen nothing with the potential to stop him from actually marrying Kanii. The woman was everything that Udoka wasn't. Kanii was kind. She also understood clearly the complex details of living with a man. She was eager, and had no reservations giving marriage a second try. Edozie knew in his heart that he had found the woman God had made just for him. And if she remained unchanged and as she had done on a daily basis, to do whatever was his bidding, he'd definitely marry her. It was the appeal that cemented his determination and kept the course of his thoughts unshakable.

Kanii had recovered from the trauma of death that constantly starred her in the face. Her life took a turn for the better, and her new family had grown into her as if she was one of them.

Six months later, the expected happened: Edozie's family gathered and blessed his relationship with the woman he had rescued from a dusty highway. That was where they left it… until Kanii's people were made to be a part of this probable union.

EPILOGUE

The world is ever-changing for better and for worse. Most cultures and customs of the world are slipping away into oblivion on a daily basis. This is true due to the slippery change itself is also predictable because of man.

Today's generation cannot survive without the use of digital devices. We have become the *Digital Natives*. The entire world is slowly drifting into one big umbrella, and the countries that have congregated there have lost their originalities and *native-ness*. This umbrella is expanding, drawing more countries in, and obliterating every bit of what makes them what and who they are.

The things that make us unique are threatened. The things that separate us, yet grant us those special identities from everyone else are on the verge of being eclipsed. Nothing is as scary as this developing phenomenon. In the foreseeable future, every corner of the world could be affected, infected by these cultural and custom disappearing acts. The world would still exist, but it could be so without any profound breath to discern where each us came from. The elegy has been written, and the polyphony from the existing meters is hence; **Tribal Echoes**, to restore hope.

Culture, customs, and the belief in one's heritage are the wholesome life that sustains any group of people, anywhere. Our heritage is the only readable DNA; the fingerprint that tells who we are. It is there in the food we eat. We live with our values everyday in our chosen works of art, as in music and the clothes we wear. Our social leanings are the product of our beliefs, even the trajectory of our minds, as in simple thought processes are rooted in our heritage. The values we preach and practice emanate from the customs and cultures we have imbibed growing up. We cannot escape it as much as some have tried to denounce and/or relegate to the background the main source of their being. When one does not embrace his or her heritage, it is simply an act of ignorance. Your heritage makes you unique.

The author of Usoro Ihenkuzi Igbo; A Practical Approach to Teaching

Igbo Language, Culture & Tradition; Benneth Okpala, said in his book: **"No culture survives without carrying a vernacular language for its intergenerational propagation. A viable and dynamic Igbo Language is needed to sustain the Igbo culture**." Isi-Ichie Benneth Okpala could not have said it better. The awareness of the importance of the Igbo language must be created in the minds of Igbo families. It is the one way to stop the loss of the Igbo culture and customs.

Until we, the Igbos, wake up from the hypnosis of Colonial conditioning, we will remain enslaved in our ignorance, and forever remain the Digital Natives.

We are the reasons stories and histories are made. As long as we are here, stories will be told of our existence; how we have, or have not carried on with the values our forefathers left for us. The chance that we could lose it all has not been foretold; but it is here. Whether we diminish our importance, by relegating our forebears' legacies, is another story.

Illustrations and Glossaries

Map of Nigeria

Map of Nigeria showing all 36 States and the 2 major Rivers

STATES, CAPITALS, AND SYMBOLS

Abuja – Federal Capital Territory (FCT), (Centre of Unity)
Abia – Umuahia (God's Own State)
Adamawa – Yola (Land of Beauty)
Akwa Ibom – Uyo (Promised Land)
Anambra – Awka (Home for All)
Bauchi – Bauchi (Pearl of Tourism)
Bayelsa – Yenagoa (Pride of the Nation)
Benue – Makurdi (Food Basket of the Nation)
Borno – Maiduguri (Home of Peace)
Cross River – Calabar (The Peoples Paradise)
Delta – Asaba (The Big Heart of the Nation)
Ebonyi – Abakaliki (Salt of the Nation)
Edo – Benin (Heartbeat of the Nation)
Ekiti – Ado-Ekiti (Fountain of Knowledge)
Enugu – Enugu (Coal City State)
Gombe – Gombe (Jewel of the Savanna)
Imo – Owerri (Land of Hope/Eastern Heartland)
Jigawa – Dutse (The New World)
Kaduna – Kaduna (Liberal State)
Kano – Kano (Centre of Commerce)
Katsina – Katsina (Home of Hospitality)
Kebbi – Birnin Kebbi (Land of Equity)
Kogi – Lokoja (Confluence State)
Kwara – Ilorin (State of Harmony)
Lagos – Ikeja (Centre of Excellence)
Nassarawa – Lafia (Home of Solid Minerals)
Niger – Minna (Power State)
Ogun – Abeokuta (Gateway State)
Ondo – Akure (Sunshine State)
Osun – Osogbo (State of the Living spring)
Oyo – Ibadan (Pacesetter State)
Plateau – Jos (Home of Peace and Tourism)
Rivers – Port Harcourt (Treasure Base of the Nation)
Sokoto – Sokoto (Seat of the Caliphate)
Taraba – Jalingo (Nature's Gift to the Nation)
Yobe – Damaturu (The Young shall grow)
Zamfara – Gusau (Farming is our Pride)

BIAFRA CURRENCY AT THE TIME OF WAR

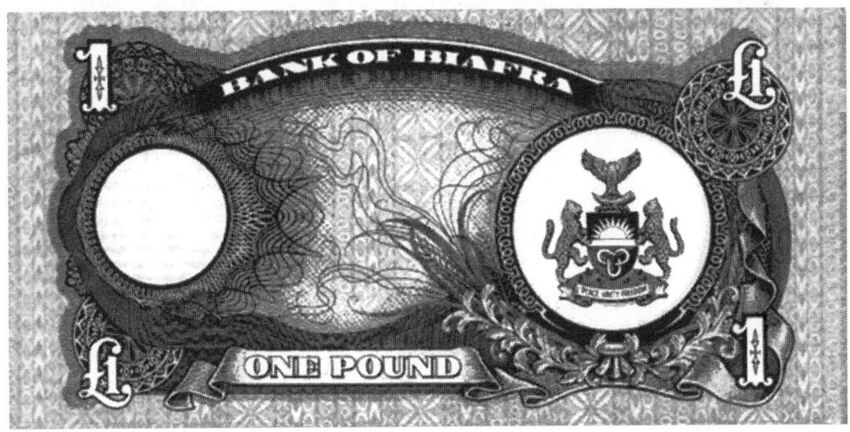

IGBO ALPHABETS

Aa	Bb	Chch	Dd	Ee	Ff	Gg	GBgb	Ghgh	Gwgw	Hh	Ii
[a]	[b]	[tʃ]	[d]	[e]	[f]	[g]	[b/g͡b]	[ɣ]	[gʷ]	[ɦ]	[i]

Ịị	Jj	Kk	Kpkp	Kwkw	Ll	Mm	Nn	Nwnw	Nyny	Ṅṅ	Oo
[ɪ]	[dʒ]	[k]	[p/k͡p]	[kʷ]	[l]	[m/m̩]	[n]	[ŋw]	[ɲ]	[ŋ]	[o]

Ọọ	Pp	Rr	Ss	Shsh	Tt	Uu	Ụụ	Vv	Ww	Yy	Zz
[ɔ]	[p]	[ɾ]	[s]	[ʃ]	[t]	[u]	[ʊ]	[v]	[w]	[j]	[z]

ROMAN NUMERIALS IN THE IGBO LANGUAGE (NON-METRIC STYLE)

One = otu
Two = abụọ
Three = atọ
Four = anọ
Five = ise
Six = isi
Seven = asaa
Eight = asatọ
Nine = itenani
Ten = iri
Eleven = iri na-otu
Twelve = iri na-abụọ
20 = ọgụ
21 = ọgụ na-otu
22 = ọgụ na-abụọ
30 (20 + 10) = ọgụ na-iri
31 = ọgụ na-iri na-otu
40 = ọgụ abụọ
41 = ọgụ abụọ na-otu
50 = ọgụ abụọ na-iri
51 = ọgụ abụọ na-iri na-otu
60 (20+20+20) = ọgụ atọ
70 (20+20+ 20+10) = ọgụ atọ na-iri
71 = ọgụ atọ na-iri na-otu
80 (20+20+20+20) = ọgụ ano
81 = ọgụ anọ na-otu
90 (20+20+20+20+10) = ọgụ anọ na-iri
100 (20x5) = ọgụ ise
1000 = puku
10,000 = puku iri
100,000 = nari puku
1,000,000 = nde
1,000,000,000 = puku nde

IGBO ALPHABETS PRONOUNCIATION GUIDE

IGBO ALPHABETS	IGBO WORDS	ENGLISH TRANSLATION	EQUAVALENT APPROXIMATE IN ENGLISH
a	aka	Hand	pat
b	- ba	Enter	box
ch	- cha	Wash	chair
d	- ndu	Life	dog
e	ego	Money	pay
f	afo	Belly	fox
g	ego	Money	get
gb	igbo	Igbo	-
gh	agha	War	-
h	ahu	Body	hat
i	isi	Head	feet
i	adiri	Line	pet
j	- je	Go	jet
k	akwa	Egg	kick
kp	akpa	Bag	-
l	ala	Land	let
m	- me	Do	mat
n	anu	Meat	net
n	anu	Bee	sing
o	- go	Buy	so
o	oji	Kolanut	more
p	- put	Go out	pet
r	iri	Ten	rat
s	isi	Head	ten
sh	isha	Crayfish	shut
t	ntu	Nail	ten
u	uchichi	Night	soon
u	ulo	House	put
w	ewu	Goat	well
y	ya	He/She/It	yet
z	azu	Fish	zebra

Male body parts in Igbo language

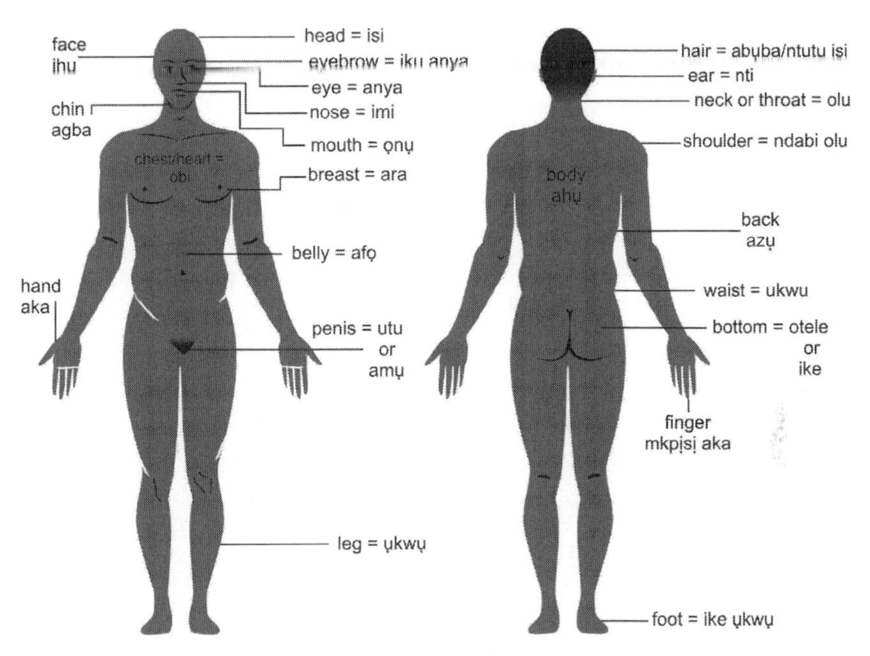

Other Body Parts

bone = ọkpụkpụ elbow = ikpere aka jaw = agba knee = ikpere ụkwụ liver = imeju
teeth/tooth = eze thumb = mkpabi aka toe = mkpịsị ụkwụ tongue = ire
vein = akwara wrist = aka kidney = akụlụ anụ/ akoro anụ

FEMALE BODY PARTS IN IGBO LANGUAGE

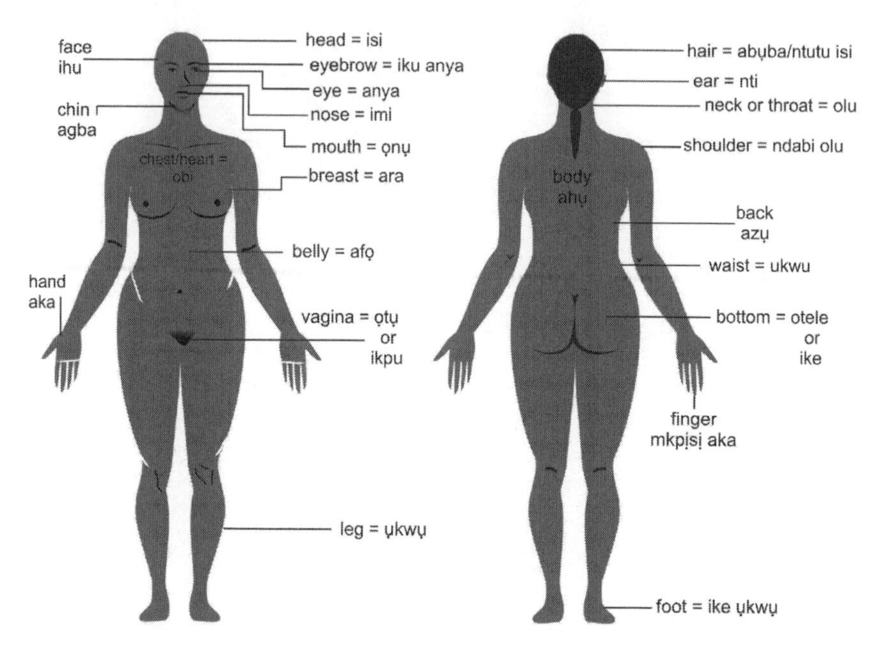

Other Body Parts

bone = ọkpụkpụ elbow = ikpere aka jaw = agba knee = ikpere ụkwụ liver = imeju
teeth/tooth = eze thumb = mkpabi aka toe = mkpịsị ụkwụ tongue = ire
vein = akwara womb = akpa ñwa wrist = aka kidney = akụlụ anụ/ akoro anụ

IGBO/ENGLISH GLOSSARY

THE UNIQUENESS OF THE IGBO LANGUAGE

A
Afternoon = **Ehihie**
Airplane = **Ụgbọ elu**
All (of us) = **Anyị n'ile**
Alcohol **= Mmanya ọkụ**
Automobile = **Ụgbọ ala**
And = **Na**
Anger **= Iwe**
Animal = **Anụmanụ**

B
Baby = **Nwa**
Bank = **Ụlọ ego**
Bad = **Ọjọọ or Njọ**
Banana = **Ogede or Une**
Beans = **Agwa**
Beauty = **Mma/Nma**
Because = **Makana**
Bed = **Akwa**
Behavior **– Agwa or Omume**
Beer = **Mmanya**
Below = **N'okpuru**
Beside = **N'akụkụ**
Big = **Nke ukwu or Ukwu**
Bike = **Ọgbatumtum**
Black = **Ojii**
Bless = **Gọzie**
Blessing = **Ngọzika**

Boat = **Ụgbọ mmiri**
Body = **Ahụ**
Book = **Akwụkwọ**
Boss = **Ọga** (Male) or **Onye isi** (Male/female)
Breakfast = **Nri ụtụtụ**
Bring = **Weta**
Broom = **Azịza**
Brother = **Nwanne** (Sibling or Maternal relative) **nwoke** (Male) = **Nwanne nwoke Nwanna** is used in reference to a paternal uncle or relative.
Bury **= ili/ili** as in a grave
Bush = **Ọhịa or ofịa**
Bush (Wild) animal = **Anụ ohịa**
But = **Mana**
Buy = **Zụta, Zụọ** or **gota**
Buyer = **Ọzụ ahia**
Bye-bye = **Kọdị or Ka ọ dịba or Naa gbuo (As in Go safely)**

C

Car = **Ụgbọ ala**
Carry = **Buru**
Cassava = **Akpụ or jiakpụ**
Center = **Etiti**
Chair = **Oche**
Chicken/Hen = **Okụkụ**
Child = **Ñwa or Ñwatakịrị**
Children = **Ụmụaka or Umụ ñtakịrị**
Christian = **Onye ụka**
Christmas = **Ekeresimesi**
Church - **Ụlọ** (House) **Ụka** (Church) = **Ụlọ ụka**
Clean = **Ọcha** (See also White) or **Ụcha**
Clock - **Elekere**
Close (As in nearby) = **Nso**
Cloth = **Akwa**
Cloud = **Urukpuru**
Coconut = **Aki oyibo** (Or, **Aki bekee**)
Cocoyam = **Ede**
Cockroach **= Ọchịcha**
Cold (As in the weather) = **Oyi**
Come = **Bịa**
Come here = **Bịa ebe a**
Cook = **Sie**

Corn/Maize = **Ọka**
Count = **Ọgụgụ**
Cow = **Ehi or Nama**
Crayfish = **Oporo**
Creator/God = **Chineke**
Cry = **Bee** (Pronunciation is not as in a bee) or **Akwa**
Customer = **Onye ahịa**

D
Dance = **Gba**
Dawn = **Ụtụtụ**
Daytime = **Ehihie**
Devil = **Ekwensu**
Do = **Mee**
Doctor = **Dibịa Oyibo**
Dog = **Nkita**
Door = **Ụzọ**
Drink = **Mmanya**
Dry Season (Fall Season) = **Ụgụrụ**
E
Early (As in dawn) = **Ụzụ ụtụtụ**
Earth = **Ụwa**
Edge = **Akụkụ**
Egg = **Akwa**
Electricity = **Ọkụ bekee/Ọkụ enu**
Elephant = **Enyi**
English = **Bekee**

F
Fall = **Ada** (To fall: **Idi ada**)
Family = **Ezi n'ụlọ**
Father = **Nna**
Finger = **Mkpịsị aka**
Fire = **Ọkụ**
First = **Mbụ**
Fish = **Azụ**
Floor = **Ala**
Food = **Nri**
Friend = **Enyi**

G

Garden eggs = **Afụfa or Mkpụrụ añara**
Girl = **Nwanyị** or **Nwata nwanyị**
Give = **Nye**
Go = **Gaa or Jee**
Goat = **Ewu**
God = **Chukwu/Chineke/Olisa**
Good = **Ọma/Mma/Nma**
Good afternoon = **Ehihe ọma**
Good behavior = **Ezi omume** (Or, **ezigbo omume**)
Goodbye = **Ka e mesịa** or **naa gboo**
Good day = **Ụbọchị ọma**
Good evening = **Abali ọma** or **uchichi ọma**
Good morning = **Ibọlachi** or **isaalachi** or **ụtụtụ ọma**
Good night = **Kachifo**
Ground = **Ala or Ani**

H

Hand = **Aka**
Hair = **Abụba isi/Ntutu**
Half = **Ọkara**
Happy - **Añụlị**
Hawk = **Egbe**
Head = **isi**
Headache = **isi mgbu or isi ọwụwa**
Hen = **Ọkụkọ**
Hold = **Jide**
Hospital = **Ụlọ ọgwụ**
Hot = **Ọkụ**
Hour = **Elekere**
House = **Ụlọ**

I

I = **Mụ** or **m** (Verb)
If = **Mana**
Inside = **N'ime**
Instead = **Kama**
It = **ọ or ya**

J

Jaw = **Agba**

Jesus Christ = **Jesu Kristi**

K
Kangaroo = **Ele**
Key – **Ọtụgwọ/Igodo**
Kill = **Gbu**
Kind = **Ụdi**
King - **Eze**

L
Land = **Ani**
Laugh = **Amụ or Ọchi**
Leaf = **Akwụkwọ**
Learn = **Mụọ**
Luggage = **Igbe or akpati**

M
Make = **Mee**
Man = **Nwoke**
Market = **Ahia**
Master = **Ọga**
Me = **Mụ or M**
Meat = **Anụ**
Medicine = **Ọgwụ**
Monkey = **Enwe**
Moon = **Ọnwa**
Morning = **Ụtụtụ**
Mother = **Nne**
Motor = **Ụgbọ ala**

N
Name = **Aha or Afa**
Next = **Ọzọ**
Night = **Abali or Uchichi**
No = **Mba**
Now = **Ugbua**

O
Occasion = **Emume**
Office = **Ụlọ ọrụ**
Oil = **Mmanụ**

Onion = **Yabasi**
Our = **Anyi**

P
Pain = **Mgbu**
Path = **Ụzọ**
Pear = **Ube**
Pepper = **Ose**
Period = **Oge**
Pig = **Ezi**
Plate = **Efere**
Please = **Biko**
Pot = **Ite**
Prayer = **Ekpere**
Pumpkin = **Ụgụ**
Pupil = **Nwata akwụkwọ**
Purchase = **Zụta**

R
Rain = **Mmiri-ozuzo**
Read/Reading = **Ọgụgụ**
Remember = **Lota**
Rice = **Osikapa**
Run = **Ọsọ/Gbaa ọsọ**

S
Sand = **Aja**
Say = **Kwuo**
School = **Ụlọ akwụkwọ**
See = **Hụ**
Sickness = **Ọria**
Since = **Ka mgbe**
Sister = **Nwanne nwanyị**
Sit = **Nọdụ anị**
Sin = **Njọ**
Small = **Ntakịrị or Ọbele**
Smart = **Amamihe**
Something = **ihe**
Son = **Ñwa nwoke**
Speak = **Kwuo**
Stick = **Osisi**

Strength = **Ike**
Sun = **Anyawụ/Anwụ**
Swim = **Gwuo**

T
Take = **Were**
Teach = **Kuzie**
Teacher = **Onye nkuzi**
Tell = **Gwa**
Thank you = **Daalụ or Imela**
That (Conjunction) = **Na or ka**
Their = **Ha**
Them = **Ha**
Then = **Mgbe ahụ**
There = **Ebe ahụ**
These = **Ndịa**
They = **Ha**

COLORS IN IGBO

Black = **Oji**
White = **Ọcha**
Red = **Mme**
Green = **Ndụ**
Yellow = **Ododo**

English Connotations/ Equivalents of Igbo Names

A

Acknowledgment (Confirmation of God's existence): **Chukwu** - God. See also **Olisa; Chukwudi or Chimdi or Nnamdi**

Affirmation (of our belief in God) - **EsomChi**

Anger or hatred (never be killed/hurt by) - **Iweobiegbunam, Iweobiegbunam (Iwobi)**

Approachable - **Dilibe**

Ask (request from or of God) - **AjuluChukwu; KanayoChukwu, AnayoChukwu, Kanayọ, Anayọ); KanayOlisa (Olisa, Kanayọ)**

B

Begging (asking God) - **KanayọChukwu (AnayọChukwu, Anayọ)**

Believe (in God) - **Esomchi**

Blessing - **AmaraChi or AmaraChukwu (Amara)**

Brave - **Dimkpa/Dike**

C

Child - **Ñwa (Child as a gift/honor) - Ginikanwa (Ginika); Nwamaka (Amaka); Nwakaego (Ego, Nwaka)**

Common sense – **Akọ, Akọbụndụ**

Companion **-Ibe, Ibeamaka**

Conscience (clear) - **Ejimọfọr; Jideọfọr; Ojiọfọr**

Consent (of God) - **IzuChukwu (Izu)**

Countless - **Ijeli**

D

Death (a plea for long life) - **Belọnwụ; Ọnwụ; Ọnwụatụegwu**

Destiny - **Chidera; Chiabụotu or Chiawụotu, Akara aka**

E

Encouragement - **Jamụike**

Enemies or Enemy - **Enewelụmokwu (Who are my enemies?)**

Enemy (in a statement: Your enemy is not your God) - **IloabụChi** (or **BụChi); IroawụChi** Enemy (plenty of)

Envy - **Iloerika**

Exemplary (Flawless, ideal, model) - **Ifeatụ or Iheatụ**

F

Faith = **Okwukwe or Nchedo**

Father - **Nna**

Father's friend - **Enyinnaya (Enyi)**

Fear (of God) - **BelụChi**

Flawless - **Ifeatụ, Iheatụ** (See also, Exemplary, Ideal, Model)

Friend - **Enyi**

Forget (never) - **EchezọnaChukwu (Echezọna)** See also Remember **(Cheta)**

G

Gift (from God) - **OsinaChi (Osy or SinaChi), IfesinaChi (Ify) Child as a gift - Ifeyinwa (Ify) Good child - Ezinwa (Ezi)**

Good luck - **Chiọma (Chi, Chi-Chi); Isiọma (Isy); Ijeọma (Ij or Ije)**

Good path - **Ezimma or Ezinma (Ezi); Ezioma (Ezi); Uzoma (Uzo)**

Goodhearted - **Obiọma**

Gossip (not to gossip/not to say bad things) - **Ekwutọsi (Ekwii or Ekwy)**

Grace- **Amara or AmaraChi (The grace of God)**

Grandfather (Paternal) - **Nnanna**

Grandmother (Paternal) - **Nnonna** (maternal) - **Nnenne**

H

Happiness - **Añụli (or Añwụli); Obiụtọ**

Heart - **Obi**

Home - **Ụnọ or ụlọ, Eruemunọ (I arrived/reached home)**

Hope - **Okwukwe**

I

Ideal - **Ifeatụ, Iheatụ** (See also, exemplary, flawless, model)

Innumerable - **Ijeli** (See also, countless, uncountable)

J

Journey - **Ije (Good journey – Ijebụsọñma, Ijeọma,** See also; **Uzọ – Path and Good path - Ụzọamaka/ Ụzọdimma/Ụzọma)**

Journey of life - Ijendụ or Ijenụwa or Ijenu

K

Kind or kindness - **Eberegbulam or Ebelegbunam (Ebere or Ebele)** (See also Mercy)

Knowing (Certainty or uncertainty) - **Amalụ (Amalụ Chukwu - Knowing God); (Who knows tomorrow? - Onyemaechi (or Amaechi)**

L

Leave - (Up to God) - **Rapụlụ Chukwu** or **Rapụlụ Olisa (**Leave it to God)

Leave (me) – **Rapụm**

Leave me alone – **Rapụm aka**

Legacy - **Ahamefula (Aham)** or **Afamefuna (Afam)**

Living (in God) - **KambirinaChi** or **KambilinaChi (Kambiri** or **Kambili)**

Life/living (Long life) - **Kwemto**

Long life (Plea) **- Belọnwụ**

Love – **Ihụnanya** or **Ifụnanya**

(The) Love of God - **IhụnanyaChukwu** or **IfụnanyaChukwu**

Love me - **Hụmnanya** or **Fụmnanya**

M

Mercy - **EbereChukwu or EbeleChukwu (Ebere or Ebele)** (See also Kind/kindness)

Miracle – **Onyinye (**As in a gift**)**

Model - (See also, exemplary, flawless, ideal) - Ifeatụ, Iheatụ

Money - **Ego**

Mother- **Nne**

N

Name - **Aha or Afa**

News - **Ozi (Ozioma = Good news)**

New - **Ọhụrụ**

Now - **Ugbua**

No - **Mba**

O

Open - **Mepeh**

Outside - **Iro**

Outsider - **Onye iro**

P

Past - **Azụ**

Patience -**Ndidi (Ndidiamaka – "Patience is a virtue")**

Peace - **Udo**

Peace (of mind) - **Obiajụlụ; Obialọ; Obielumani**

Possibility **(Impossible with God) – IfeanyiChukwu; Ifeanyi)**

Power **(of God) – IkeChukwu, IkeChi or Ikenna**

Power **(in God) - IkedinaChi or IkedinaChukwu**

Power **(of prosperity) - Ikemefuna (My strength should not be in vain)**

Praise **(to God) - SomtoChukwu, EtoChukwu, KeneChukwu, KeleChi or KeneChi or Kenenna or KeneChukwu, ToChukwu/ TobeChukwu/Tobenna, DumetoChukwu, DumetOlisa (Dumeto or Olisa); EkenediliChukwu (Ekene), KwemtoChukwu (Kwemto)**

Precious – **Adakụ, Adaugo, Adanma, Akwaugo, Ọlaedo, Ugonna, Ugodiya, Ugonna or UgoChukwu**

Priceless – **Adaugo, UgoChukwu**

Princess - **Adaeze**

Protection - **Anichebem, Nnachebem or Chizobam**

R

Rejoice - **Golieh or ñulia (See Anuli)**

Remember - **Echezona or Lota (As in EchezonaChukwu or Lotanna)**

Respect **(of God) - BeluChi**

Riches - **AkuChukwu, Akuzie, Akumbu, Akuabata, Akuabia, Akumjeli, or Akunna**. See also Wealth

S

Satisfaction - **Abazu**

Say (to say or not to say) - **Ekwutọsi (Not to gossip or say bad things)**

Strength or Strong - **Dike or Ike**

T

Take things easy - **Ejikemeifeuwa or Emenike**

Thank (to God) (See also Praise God) - **DumetoChukwu, DumetOlisa**

Time (God's time) - **Ogechukwu or OgeChi (Oge)**

Trust (in God) - **Anenechukwu (Anene) or KaneneChukwu (Kani)**

U

Uncountable - **Ijeli (**See also, **countless, innumerable)**

Up (to God) – **EleChi, EleweChi or EneweChi**

V

Victory (of the brave) - **Ebube Dike**

W

War **(A child born during a war) - Ijeagha, Chiwetalundu or Aghadi**

Wealth - **Akụmbụ, Akụabata, Akụabia, Akụmjeli, Akụnna, Obiageli, and Obianuju**

Wish **(Good wishes) - Obiọha or Obiọra (The wishes of the people/ community)**

Wish **(of God) – Obinna and Longing wish: Iheanachọ or Ifeanachọ or wishing a safe journey: Ijeọma or wishing for something good: Ifeọma, Iheọma or Ihuọma.**

Igbo Names And Their Unique Meanings

The meanings and translations of these names as depicted below, are not soley that of the author's

Many Igbos believe in oneness through God. Therefore, most of the Igbo names are reflections of the image, strength, grace, and the totality of God.

Some of the most common words associated with Igbo names are as follow:

Chi = God, god, Guiding light, Guardian angel or Spirit
Chukwu/Chineke/Olisa = God
Nna = God, Father in Heaven, father/dad
Amaka = Beautiful, great, good, amazing, wonderful
Nwa = Child/baby
Nwanne = Brotherhood/sisterhood
Nne = Mother
Nma/Mma = Beautiful/beauty, goodness or niceness
Obi = Heart

Note:

The letter **'m'** when used at the end of a name personalizes the plea for… for instance, Chidube**m (**Meaning: **God, lead me** compares to saying; Chidube which **God leads)**

Most or all the names shortened are in parenthesis. The DIGITAL NATIVES have continually short-formed some or most of these native names in an effort to appear more Western and/or marketable. However, the meanings of these names are ever the same.

Each name is tagged **'m'** = male and/or **'f'** = female.

A

Abazu (m) - You never get rich enough (be contempt with your blessings).

Achebe (m) - Full name could be Anichebem meaning: May the land or the land deity protect me; Chichebem or Nnachebem meaning: May God protect me; Chebe simply means to protect.

Adaeke (f) - A female child born on Eke market day (Ada)

Adaeze or Adaezennaya or Adaobi (f) - A princess or the first daughter of prominent man (King = Igwe). Or simply a man who considers himself of a prominent status) (Ada)

Adakụ (f) - Precious or treasured daughter (Ada)

Adanma or Adamma (Ada or Nma) (f) - Beautiful/precious/treasured daughter

Adaọra (f) - Daughter of the people (Ada)

Adaugo/Akwaugo (f) - Ugo means an Eagle which signifies purity, excellence or delicacy Akwa means Egg. **Adaugo (Ada)** means the excellent daughter

Adaure (f) or Urenma – Pride of the first daughter or Pride in beauty (Goodness)

Afamefuna or Ahamefula (m) - May my name, legacy never vanish/ disappear (as in having a male son). Simply means the importance of a male child in Igboland for the continuation of the family name.

Afụlụenu (f) - The sky is too high to be seen

AfọmaChukwu (f) - The grace or mercy of God (Afọma)

AjụlụChukwu (m) - I /We asked God (Ajụlụ)

Alaọma (f) - Good land (Ọma)

Akabụeze (m) See also Akụbụeze

AkaChi (m) - God's hands (See also KaọdinakaChi)

AkaOlisa (m) - The handwork of God (Akọsa or Akọ)

Akọbụndụ (m) - Common sense is essential for survival (Ndụ)

Akọma (f) - Goodluck (Ọma)

Akụabia (f) - Wealth, treasure or riches have come (Akụ)

Akụbụeze (m) - Wealth is king (The power of wealth)

Akụbụndụ (m) - Akụ means wealth; Ndụ means life. So…wealth is life (Akụ or Ndụ)

AkụChukwu (f) God's wealth (Akụ)

Akụdinobi (m/f) - Wealth is in the mind/heart (Dinobi).

Akụkalia (f) - Surplus wealth (Akụ or Kalia)

Akụmbụ (f) - First wealth (Akụ)

Akụkọdi (m/f) - There is a story. For instance; a child born in the midst of calamity could be named Akụkọdi (Kọdi)

Akụmjeli (f) - My wealth/treasure I will enjoy (Akụ)

Akụnna (f) - Father's wealth (Akụ)

Akwaugo (f) - Akwa = egg; Ugo = Eagle; A precious child (Ugo)

Agbọnma (f) - Beautiful girl (Nma)

Amaechi or Amechi (m) - Echi means tomorrow. See also Onyemaechi

Amaefule or Amaefuna (m/f) - Never lose your roots. See also Ahamefula or Ahamefuna

Amadi (male) - A strong man or a deity or someone that is not tagged an "Osu;" a freeborn.

Amaka (f) - Something/someone good or beautiful. See also Nwamaka, Chiamaka, Ụzoamaka or Ụkamaka

AmalụChukwu (m/f) - knowing God (Amalu)

AmaraChi or AmaraChukwu (f) - God's blessing or the grace of God (Amara)

AmaucheChukwu or Amauchenna (f) - Who knows the Will or the mind of God! (Amauche or Uche) See also UcheChukwu or Uchenna (m/f)

Amazilo (f) - I do not know all my enemies (Ama)

AmogeChukwu (f) - No one knows God's time (Amoge or Oge or OgeChi). See also AmucheChukwu, Amuchenna

AnayọChukwu or AnayOlisa (m) – Let's keep asking God… See also KanayọChukwu and KanyinayọChukwu

AneneChukwu or AneneChi (m/f) - Let us believe/trust in and look up to God (Anene or Annie)

Añụlika (f) Happiness is greater (Anuli)

ArinzeChukwu (m) - The grace of God (Arinze)

Awele See also Ijeawele

Azikiwe (m) - It is better to be angry than to be hateful. Azi means hate. Iwe means anger or state of being annoyingly agitated (Zik)

Azụbụike (m) - Azụ means back or backwards/past. Ike means strength. The past is your strength. Experience is the best teacher. (Azụ or Ike)

Azụka (m/f) - It is almost same as Azụbụike. One's past experience should be a learning experience (Zukky)

Azụmeh or Azụmme (m/f) - The past is behind us (Azụ)

B

BelụChi (m) – Cry out to God (Belụ)

Belọnwụ or Balọnwụ (m) - Ọnwụ means death; an acknowledgement of the inevitability of death. It simply means a plea for long life.

BụChi (m/f) - See also OnyebụChi, IbeabụChi or MadụabụChi

BaChinobi (m) – Enter into God's heart (BaChi)

C

ChelụChi (f) - Wait on God (Chi)

Chekwube (f) - Rely on God (Chi)

ChetaChi (f/m) - Remember God (Cheta or Chi)

Chiabụotu or Chiawotu (m/f) - Literally means that though we are the same in oneness of God, our destinies are different because we have different spirits (Chi or Chichi)

Chiagọziem (m/f) - God has blessed me (Chi, Agọziem or Gọziem)

Chiahalam (m/f) - Symbol of a plea for the mercy of God. Literally means may God never forsake me. (Chi for m/f or Chichi for f)

Chialụka or Chieloka (m) - God has done a great deed (Alụka or Eloka)

Chiamaka (f) - God is beautiful/great (Chi or Amaka)

Chiazagomekpere (m/f) - God has answered my prayer (Chi or Chiazagom). See also Chinazaekpere

Chibụeze (m) - God is king (Chi)

Chibugo (m/f) - God is pure (Chi or Ugo)

Chibụọgọ (f) - God is gracious (Chichi or Ọgọ)

Chibụsọnma (f) - God is full of beauty (Sọnma)

Chibụzọ (m/f) - God is the leader (Chi, Chichi or Uzọ)

Chidaalụ (m/f) - Thank you God (Daalụ). See also DaalụChi

Chidi (m/f) - There is God. It is same as Chukwudi or Chimdi (Chi or Chụdi)

Chidera (f) - It is same as Olisadera (m/f). When God has written, it must come to pass (When God say yes (no), no man can say no (yes)) (Dera, Ọdera or Chi)

Chidiebere or Chidiebele (m/f) - God is gracious or merciful (Chidi, Chi or Ebere)

Chidiegwu (m) - God is great (Chidi)

Chidinma or Chidimma (f) - God is good (Chidi, Chi or Chichi)

Chidubem (m) - It is same as Chinedum (m/f) God guides me (Chi (m/f), Dubem, Edu or Dumdum (m))

Chidumebi (f) - God lives with me (Dumebi) See also Chisomebi

Chidumaga (m/f) - My God is with me or my God leads me (Chi or Chichi)

Chidozie or Chiedozie (m) - God mends or God has preset… (Chido or Dozie)

Chiebuka (m) - The totality of God is immeasurable (Ebuka)

Chiefo (m) - Dawn of the day (Chi)

Chiedozie (m) - God has done great (Edozie of Dozie)

Chiekwugo (m/f) - God has spoken (Chi or Chichi)

Chieloka (m) - The depths of God's thoughts are immeasurable. (Chi, Chichi or Eloka)

Chiemeka (m) - God has done something amazingly wonderful (Chi or Emeka). See also Chukwuemeka and Nnaemeka

Chiemenam (m/f) - God will never harm or be against me. See also Chizobam (Chi or Chichi)

Chiemela (m/f) - God has done it; something wonderful (Chi or Chichi)

Chiemelie (m/f) – God is victorious (the battle); defeated Satan (Chi or Emelia)

Chiemezie (m/f) - God has done (mended/fixed) the impossible (Chi or Mezie)

Chineze (f) - God protects (Chine). See also Chizobam

Chienezie (m/f) - God has taken care of (someone/something) graciously/favorably (Chi or Nezie)

Chiganụ (m) - God will answer (Affirmation of faith in God) (Chi)

Chigbogu (m) - God settles fights/differences. (Chi, Chigbo or Ogbọgụ)

Chigọlụm (m/f) - God will fight/plead for my innocence (Chi or Chigọ)

Chigoziem or Chiagoziem (m/f) - God bless me or God has blessed me

Chijindụm (m/f) - God owns and has my life or God determines the end of my life (Chi, Chiji or Ndụ)

Chijioke (m) - God is the giver of blessings (Chi or Chiji)

Chikadibia or Chukwukadibia (m) - God is greater than the seer of a deity (Chi, Chuka or Chika)

Chikamara (f) - God knows better… (Chika or Amara)

Chikaemele (f) - It is God I look up to (Chika)

Chike (m) - The power/strength of God (Chi)

Chikelụ or Chikere/Chukwukere (m) - God creates/created (Chi)

Chikezie (m) - A plea for God's fair judgment (Chi, Chike, Okezie or Kezie)

Chikeziri (m) - God had created/apportioned well or greatness

Chikọdili (f) - It is up to God (Chichi, Chi, Chikọ or Kọdili)

Chikosi (f) - This (gift) is from God (Chi or Kosi)

Chikwado (m/f) - God approves… (Chi or Chichi)

Chikwendụ (m/f) - God is the provider of life (Chi or Chichi)

Chikwube (m) - God says or will say (Chi or Kwube)

Chimaijem (m/f) - God knows my path (steps/journey) (Chichi, Chi, Chima (m) or Ijem)

Chimamanda (f) - My God will never fail (Chi or Amanda)

Chimaobim (m) - God knows my heart (Chima or Maobim)

Chimaoke or Chimaraoke (m) - God knows (my) share (Chima)

Chimerebere (f) - The mercy of God (Chime or Ebere)

Chimdaalụ (m/f) - Thank you my God. Daalụ means thank you (Chimda)

Chimdi (m/f) - My God is (lives) (Chi or Chidi). See also Chidi or Chukwudi

Chimdinma (f) - My God is good (Chi). See also EsomsinaChimdinma

Chimelụọgọ (f) - God was gracious (Chi or Ọgọ or Ọmelụọgọ)

Chimezie (m/f) See also Chidozie

Chimsom (f) - My God is/lives with me (Chi or Chichi). See also Chisom and Mụnachiso

Chimzimụzọ (f) - My God, show me the way (Chimzi or Ụzọ)

Chinagọrọm (m/f) - God is aware of and will fight for my innocence. (Chi, Chichi or Agọrọm)

Chinazamekpere or Chinasaekpere (f) - God answers (my) prayers (Chi, Chinaza, or Chinasa or Ekpere). Ekpere means prayer(s)

Chinecherem (f) - God's has thoughts for me or God watches over me (Chi or Echerem)

Chinedum (m/f) - God leads me…to the right path. (Chi (m/f), Chine (f), Nedu (m) or Edu/Dumdum (m))

Chinekwu (f) - God decides/says/determines (one's fate) (Chi or Chine)

Chinelo (f) - The Will of God (good wishes) (Chichi or Nelo)

Chinemeremma (f) - God blesses me graciously (Chi or Chineme)

Chinenye (f) - God provides… (Chichi or Nenye)

Chineze (f) - God protects (Chi)

Chinọmso or Chinọnso (m/f) - God is near/with me (Chi or Nọnso or Nọmso)

Chinọnyelụm (f) - God be with me (Nọnie, Nọnye or Nọnyelụm)

Chinụaekpere (f) - God, hear (my/our) prayers (Chinụa)

Chinweike (f) - God has the power (Chinwe)

Chinwemma or Chinwenma (f) - God is beauty therefore, owns beauty (Chinwe or Nma)

Chinwem (f) - God owns me (Chinwe)

Chinwendụ (f) - God has the power for the gift of life (Chinwe)

Chinweụba (m) - The power of wealth belongs to God (Nweụba)

Chinwizu (f) - God has the plan (Chi or Nwizu)

Chinwoke (f) or Chijioke (m/f) - God determines (my/our) shares of blessings (Chinwe, Chi, or Chioke)

Chinyere or Chinyelụ (f) - God gives (Chichi). See also Chinenye

Chiọma (f) - Good God (Chichi)

Chisom (m/f) - (Or, Chisomebi (f)) God is with me or God lives with me (Chi (m/f), Somebi (f) or Soso (f))

Chiwetalụ (ndụ = life) (m) - God brings (life) (Chi)

Chizaram (f) - God has answered me (Zara)

Chizitelụm (f) - God brought me (Chichi or Chizi)

Chizimụzọ (f) - God, show me the way (Chizi or Zimụzọ or Ụzọ)

Chizọbam or Chizọba (m/f) - God saves or protects me (Chichi, Chi or Zọbam)

Chizuoke (m/f) - God is perfect (Chi)

Chukwualụka or Chialụka (m) - God has done a great deed (Chi or Alụka)

Chukwubụikem or Chibụikem (m) - God is my strength (Chi or Ikem)

Chukwudi (m) - Affirmation of God's existence (Chudi or Chidi)

Chukwuebuka (m) - God is great (Chi or Ebuka)

Chukwueloka or Chieloka (m) - The greatness and depths of God's counsel (Eloka)

Chukwuemeka or Nnaemeka (m) - God has done a great deed (Emeka)

Chukwufụmnanya (m) or IfụnanayaChukwu (f) - God loves me or the love of God - (Chi, Ify or Fụmnanya)

Chukwuhaenye or Chukwuraenye (m) - God decides (Chi)

Chukwujamụike or Chijamụike (m) - God, give me strength (Chi or Jamụike)

Chukwujekwu or Chigekwu (f) - It's up to God or God decides (Chichi)

Chukwukadibia (m) See also Chikadibia

Chukwukere (m) See also Chikere or Chikelụ

Chukwuma (m) See also Chima or Chuma

Chukwumaobim (m) See also Chimaobim (Obim or Maobim or Maobi)

Chukwumalụoge or Chimalụoge (f) - God knows His time (Chimalụ or Oge). See also OgeChi

Chukwunọnso (m) See also Chinọnso (m/f)

D

DaalụChi or DaalụChineke (f) - Thank you God (Daalụ). See also Chidaalụ

DebereChi (f) - Leave it (your worries or expectations) up to God (Chi or Debere)

Dike (m) - A brave/strong man

Dilibe or Diribe (m) - May you be of good model to your peers (Dili or Ibe)

Dinobi (m) - It is in the heart (Din or Obi)

DumtoChukwu, DumtOlisa, DumkeneChi or SoromtoChi (m) - Join me and praise God (Dumto, Kene or ToChi). See also SolumtobeChukwu, SomkeneChukwu, SomtoChukwu or Somgolie

E

EbeleChukwu or EbereChukwu (m/f) - The mercy of God; Ebele or Ebere means mercy (Ebere, Ebele or Eby) See also Chimerebere

Ebelemgbulam or Eberemgbulam (m/f) - May my kindness or goodness never harm me or returned for evil (Ebere, Eby or Ebele)

EchezọnaChukwu (m) - Never forget God. (Eche or Echezọna)

Echika (m/f) - Tomorrow is greater.

Egobụdike (m) - Money makes a man (Dike)

Egoliem (f) - I rejoice (Ego)

Egondụ (f) - The wealth of life (Ego)

Ejikemeuwa (m) - Take the things of life, easy (Ejike or Ejikeme)

Ejimọfọr Similar to Jideọfọr (m) - My conscience is clear (Ejii)

Ejimone (m) - How many do I have? (Ejim)

EkeChukwu (m) - God cannot be created

EkenediliChukwu/EkenChi or Ekenedilinna (m) - All praises to God (Ekene) See also KeneChi, KeleChi or Kenenna

Ekwueme or Okaome (m) - Keep to your promise/action speaks louder than words. (Ekwy)

Ekwutọsi (f) - Avoid saying or simply do not say bad things about others (Ekwii or Ekwy)

EleChi or EleweChi (m/f) - Look up to God (Trust God)

Eluemụnọ (m/f) - I am home (Eluem)

Emeka (m) - See also Chiemeka, Chukwuemeka or Nnaemeka

Emeremgini (m/f) - What did I do? (Emerem)

Emenike (m) - Similar to Ejikemeifeuwa Take things easy

Enemuo (m) - Beware or avoid the sight of evil/spirit

Enwelumokwu (f) - I have something to say or an opinion

Enyinnaya (m) - A friend of his father's. See also Ogbonnaya. (Enyi)

SoChi or SoroChi (f) - Follow God or Only God (depending on the pronunciation/dialect)

Eso/m/si/na/Chi/m/di/nma (f) - I am among those that praise God or acknowledge the goodness of God. (Esom, Somsi, Dina, Chimdi, or Nma)

Erinma (f) - The beautiful one or the epitome of beauty. (Eri or Nma)

EtoChi or EtoChukwu (m) - When you praise God… He blesses you more (Eto or ToChi)

Eziafakaego (f) - Good name is better than money (Ezi)

Ezije (m/f) - Good path. See also Uzoma and Ijeabalum

Ezigbom (m/f) - My love

Ezimma or Ezinma (f) - Good community. Ezi means path; nma means good. See also Uzọma (Zim or Nma)

Ezinne (f) Good mother - (Ezi or Nne) See also Nneka. Nne means mother.

Ezinwa (m/f) - A good child: Nwa means a child.

Eziọma (f) - Good community or safe place outside

F

Fụmnanya (f) Love me. See also Ifụnanya

FebeChukwu (m/f) -Worship God (FebeChi or Febe)

G

Ganiru (f) - Go forward. See also Sọniru

Ginikanwa (f) - What is greater than a child? See also Nwamaka (Ginika)

GinikaChi (m/f) – What is greater than God?

Golibe or Goliwe (m/f) - Rejoice (Golie)

Gwamniru (f) - Say it to my face

Gọzie (m) - Bless See also Chigọzie or Chiagọzie

H

Halim (f) - Leave me alone (Hali) See also RapụlụChukwu

HanyeChukwu or HanyeOlisa (f) - (NyeChi) Leave it up to God. See also RapụlụChukwu or RapụlụOlisa

I

Ibeamaka (m) - Companionship is good. (Three is not a crowd; the more the merrier in a joyous event) (Ibe)

IbeabụChi (m) – None is God. See also MadụabụChi and OnyebụChi. (BụChi or Ibe)

Ibekwe (m) – The consent of my people (Ibe)

Ibezimakọ (m) – My people have shown me wisdom. (Ibe or Ibezim)

Ifeanachọ (m) - See also Iheanacho. What I have been hoping, wishing, asking, waiting or looking for (Ify)

IfeanyiChukwu (m/f) With God, all things are possible. (Ify or Ifeanyi)

Ifeatụ (m) - An ideal model or a comparison to…(a benchmark). See also Iheatụ.

Ifenemonye (m) - What happens to a person…!

Ifeọma (f) - Something good (Ifey, Ify, or Ifọ). See also Iheọma

Ifesinachi (m/f) - It (gift) is from God. See also OsinaChi (Ify)

Ifeyinwa (f) - There's no gift like a child (Ifey or Ify)

IfụnanyaChukwu (f) - The love of God. Ifụnanya means love. See also Fụmnanya (Ify)

Igwebụike (m) - Two or more are greater. There is strength in unity.

Iheatụ (m) - See also Ifeatụ

Iheanachọ (m) - See also Ifeanachọ

Iheọma (f) - See also Ifeọma

Ihuọma (m/f) - Good aura (the face has) or the future is brighter (Ọma). See also Uzọma

Ijeagha (m/f) - The journey of war (Especially; a child born during the war) (Ije or Agha)

Ijeabalụm (f) - The journey favored me. (Ij or Ije)

Ijeoyiboamaka (f) - The journey to the White man's world is a beautiful blessing (Ij, Ije or Oyibo or Amaka)

Ijeamaka (f) - A safe journey or a good path to a destination. See also Ụzọma or Ụzọamaka

Ijeawele or Ijengala (f) - The walk of pride (Ije or Awele). See also Awele

Ijebụsọmma (f) - The journey is good (Ije or Sọmma). See also Ijeọma

Ijeli (m/f) - Countless

Ijendụ (m/f) - The walk/journey of life (Ije (f) or Ndu (m)) See also Ijeoma

Ijenụwa (f) - The amazing path to or journey of life (Ije or Ijenu)

Ijeọma (m/f) - Safe journey. This name is pronounced differently depending on the sex (Ij or Ije). See also Ijendụ, Ụzọdinma, Ụzọamaka and Ụzọma

IkeChukwu or IkeChi (m) - The power or strength of God (Ike or Iyke). See also Ikenna

IkedinaChukwu (m) - There is power in the God. (Ike or Ikedi)

Ikemefuna (m) - May my strength never be lost (Ikem or Efuna). See also Ahamefula or Afamefuna

Ikenna (m) - The power of God (Ike or Iyke). See also Ikechukwu

Iloabachie (m) - Enemity abounds (Abachie)

IloabụChi (m) - Literally meaning: Your enemy is not God (AbụChi or BụChi)

Iloerika (m/f) - Enemies are numerous (Erika)

Isioma (f) - Good luck (Isy). See also Chima

Iweobiegbulam or Iweobiegbunam (m) - May sadness, heartache, anger, or hatred not harm or overwhelm me. (Iwobi or Obi)

IzuChukwu or Izunna (m) - The (secret) plan of or God (Izu)

Izukanmananneji (m) - Secrets are concealed by your blood (siblings of same father and mother). (Izu or Nneji)

J

Jamuike (m) - Encourage or praise me (Ike)

Jeneta or Jenete (f) - Go and be (see as…) a witness to something good or a news or a miracle (Neta, Eta or Ete)

Jideọfọr (m) - Jide means to have or to hold and Ọfọr in Igbo land symbolizes the staff of truth or peace. When someone says that that he or she jide ofor for you, it means that the person possesses the "ofor" should and must have a clear impeccable conscience in the situation to avoid nemesis. See also Ojiọfọr, Ejimọfọr or Ọfọdili.

K

Karanne (f) - Tell mother (Kara or Nne)

KaraChi (f) - Tell God (Kara)

Kasiemobi or Kasirimobi (m/f) - Console my heart. (Kasie (m/f) or Mobi (m))

KamaraChi (f) - Let me know God/I will know God. (Kamara)

KamalụChukwu (m) - Let me know God/I will know God. (Kamal)

KambinaChi or KambirinaChi or KambilinaChi (m/f) - I am living in or let me live in God (Kambina, Kambili or Kambiri)

Kamdibe (m/f) - I will deal with it patiently. (Dibeh)

Kameme (m/f) - My hard work is never good enough

Kamnolue (m/f) - I will stay or allow me to stay (Kammy)

KamsiyọChukwu (f) - How I asked God! (Kamsi)

KanayoChukwu (m/f) - We will keep asking/begging God. (Kanayo (m/f) and Anayo (m))

KaneneChi (f) - Let's be looking up to God (Kanene or Kanii)

Kanụ or Kalụ (m) - A sacred deity

Kanyiñụlia (f) - Let us rejoice (Ñụlia)

KanyitoChukwu or KanyitoChi or Kanyitonna (m) - Let praise God. (ToChi, Tonna)

KanyirayoChukwu (f) - How many we are that asked God (Kaira)

Kaodilinye (m/f) - To keep company or remain with (Dili)

KaodinakaChi (m) - We leave it in God's hands (Ọdy, Ọdinaka, and AkaChi)

Ka/onye/gwa/Chie - Whatever one tells his/her God.

KeleChi (m/f) - Thank God. Kene or Kele means thank. It is same as

KeneChi, Kenenna, or KeneChukwu (Kele, Kene or Ken). See also EkenediliChukwu or Ekenedilinna

KobeluChukwu (m) - It ends with God or it is up to God how it ends (Kobelu)

KobiChukwudi (m) - How God's heart is...nothing compares (Koby or KobiChi)

KodiliChukwu (m/f) - It is up to God (Kody (m), Dili (f) Kodili (m/f)). It is same as KodilinyeChukwu

KosisọChukwu (m/f) - However it pleases God (Kosy or Kosisọ)

Kwemto (m) - A plea to praise

KwemtoChukwu (m) - Allow me to praise God (Kwemto)

L

LotaChukwu or Lotanna (f) - Remember God (Lota or LotaChi)

M

MadụabụChi (m) - No one is God (AbuChi or BuChi). See also IbeabụChi

Madụkaife (m) - Man is greater than all things (Maduka)

Madụkaego (m) - A human being is worth more than money (Madụka)

Madụeke (m) - Man is not the creator

Madụekwe (m) - Man disagrees

Madụkwe (m) - Man agrees

MakọaChukwu (m) - Embrace (hold on to) God (Makọa)

Mụọmelu (m) - God (the Spirit) did (the amazing).

Mbadiwe (m) - An angry people or town

Mbanefo (m) - Upcoming people

Mgbafọr (f) - A female born on Afor market day

Mgbankwọ (f) - A female child born on Nkwo market day

Mgborie (f) - A female child born on Orie market day

MmaOlisa (f) - The beauty of God (Mma)

MmesọmaChukwu (f) - The blessings (or the grace) of God (Mmeso or Sọma)

Mụkọsọ (f) - This (it) pleases me

MụnaChiso (m/f) - God and I are one. Basically, God is with me (Muna)

MụnaChimso (m/f) - My God and I are one (Muna)

N

Ndidiamaka (f) - Perseverance is rewarding (Ndidi, Ndy or ND). "Patience is a virtue."

Ndụbụagha (m) - Life is a struggle (Ndụ, ND or Agha)

Ndụbụeze (m) - Life is sacred (king) (Ndụ or ND)

Ndụbụisi (m) - Life is the ultimate. "Isi" means head. Practically, what is the rest of your body without your head? (Ndụ or ND)

Ndụdi (m) - If there is life then… (Ndụ or ND)

Ndụkakụ (m) - Life is better than wealth. (Ndụka, Ndụ or ND)

Ndụlụ or Nduru (f) - A dove (A symbol of beauty) (ND)

NebeChi or NebeChukwu or NebeOlisa (m) Look up to God. (Nebe)

Nebeụwa (m) - Observe the world (and basically see what it has in store) (Nebe).

Ngalakwesi (f) - Pride befits (One) (Ngala)

Ngoli (f) - To be in a joyous mood or rather, to simply show off (with pride)

NgoziChukwuka (m/f) - The blessings of God are immeasurable. Ngozi means blessing. (Ngozi (m/f), N.G or Ngo (f), Chuka (m))

Nkadi (m/f) - A plea for something or someone to be (to live) See also Ozoemena

NkeChinyerem (f) - The gift/one (someone or something) God has given (or will give). (NkeChi, Nky, Niki or N.K)

Nkediniruka or Nkemdiniruka (f) - The future is greater. (Nkee or Iruka) See also Nkeiruka See also Nkiruka

Nkemakọlam or Nkemakọnam (m/f) - A plea for prosperity. May I never be found not wanting or lack… (Nkem)

Nkemdiniruka (f) - My future is greater. Nkem means mine (something or someone that belongs to you). Therefore, it can also serve as a pet name. (Nkem, Nkemdi or Iruka)

NkemdinaChi (f) - My path/future is with God. (Nkem or DinaChi)

Nkemdilim or Nkemdirim (m/f) - A plea for stability/may mine remain the same. (Nkem)

Nkemjika (m/f) or **Njideka (f)** - This refers to a child; probably after a long awaited hope of conception/birth of a child. It also practically means that "a bird at hand is worth more than two in the bush." (Nkem, Nkemji or Njide or Jideka)

Nkemka (f) - Mine is greater (Nkem or Kemka)

Nkem/na/agum (f) - I long for what is mine (Nkem)

Nkili/eji/afọ (f) - One never gets tired of admiring a thing of beauty. (Nkili)

Nkiruka (f) - The future looks brighter and is the best to come. (Nkiru, Nikki or Iruka)

Nkọlika (f) - It is better to be optimistic than pessimistic. (Nkoli)

Nkonye (f) - What belongs to one (you). (n)

Nnagoziem (m) - God has blessed me (Nna or Agoziem). See also Chiagoziem.

Nnabụife or Nnaife (m) - Father is worth a lot (Nna). See also Nwanyib□ife

Nnabụikem (m) - God is my strength. (Ikem)

Nnachetam or Nnacheta (m) - God remember me.

Nnaeto (m) - I am full of praise (Nnaeto) - See also Obimnaeto

Nnaemeka (m) - God has done a great/wonderful thing (Emeka). See also Chiemeka, Chukwuemeka, and Olisaemeka.

Nnamdi (m) - This name can go either my father lives (God) or a son named after or as a symbol of his father, or, as a reincarnation of his grandfather (Nna or Nna m).

Nnamụtaezinwa (m/f) - A father has a good child… (…to love) (Nna)

Nnanna (m) - Grandfather (Nnanna). An example would be when a male child is assumed to reincarnate or is a symbol of his grandfather.

Nneamaka (f) - A mother is a thing (symbol of motherhood) is beauty (Nne or Amaka)

Nneka (f) - Mother is great (Nne or Eka)

Nnenna (f) - Maternal grandfather. When a female child is believed to reincarnate her father's mother (Nne)

Nnenne (f) - Maternal grandmother; this when a female child is believed to reincarnate her mother's mother (Nne)

Nneoma (f) - Good mother (Nne). See also Ezinne.

Nnonso (m/f) - See also Chinonso or Chinomso.

Nwabude (f) - Nwa means a child, bụ means is and ude means a sound (happy or unhappy sound). A child is the sound for happiness.

Nwabụnọ (m/f) - The joy of a child completes a home.

Nwabugwu (m/f) - The pride of a child or a child is one's pride.

NwaChinemelu (m) - Someone (not necessarily a child) who is blessed by God (NwaChi)

NwaChukwu (m) - A child of God (NwaChi)

NwaChikwelụndụ (m) - The child that God has promised life (NwaChi or Chikwelụndụ)

Nwadimkpa (m) - A child is important (Nwadi)

Nwadiụtọ or Nwasọka (f) - A child is sweet or the sweetness or the joy of a child (Nwadi)

Nwagugheụzọ (m) - May this child be a door to more blessings. (Nwagụ)

Nwakaego or Nwakego (f) - A child is more valuable than money (Nwaka or Kego, Ego)

Nwakasi (f) - A child is priceless (Nwaka)

Nwakanma (f) - A child is better acquisition than anything (as a preference) (Kanma). See also Nwakaego

Nwalibeakụ (f) - A child should enjoy riches. See also Ọbiageliakụ

Nwalibe (f) - A child should eat or enjoy! (Libe)

Nwamaka (f) - A child is precious. (Amaka) See also Ifeyinwa.

Nwando (f) or Nwa/muru/na/ndo (m/f) - See also Nwabụndo

Nwabụndo (f) - A child is refuge or peace

Nwannedimma (f) - Family or sibling is important. (Nwanne or Nnedi)

Nwaenefuru (f) - The neglected or lost child (Efuru)

Nwanneka (m/f) - Family/brotherhood/sisterhood is supreme. (Nwanne (m/f) and Nneka (f))

Nwankwọ (m) - A male child born on "Nkwo" market day

Nwanyibụife (f) - A woman (female) has a great value. It is also an expression of a yearning for a male child (Bụife)

Nwebube (m) - A miraculous son (Ebube)

Nweke (m) - A male child born on "Eke" market day

Nwokeọcha (m) - Light-complexioned male

Nwokezuike (m) - A strong energetic man or could refer as a man who never rests; always working hard

Nwokike (m) - A child of creation (Okike)

Nworie or Nwoye (m) - A male child born on "Orie" market day

Nwọra (m) - A child of the community. See also Obiọra

Nwụlari (f) - Ụlari means Silk; 100% silk is simply soft and beautiful. Nwụlari is like a child of silk

O

Obiamaka (f) - The beautiful heart (Amaka)

Obianika (m) - The heart endures (or endured) (Obi or Anika)

Ọbiageli (f) – The one born into wealth (Oby). See also Ọbianuju

Obiajụlụ or Obialọ (m/f) - The heart is at peace or consoled. This is the issue of a long awaited child. (Obi (m) and Ajụlụ (m/f))

Ọbianuju (f) or Ọbialụ (m) - The one (basically a child) who came in the midst of abundance and should not face poverty (Oby). See also Obiageli

Obianwụ (m) - The heart (the spirit) never dies (Obi)

Obidimkpa (m) - The heart a brave man (Obi)

Obielumani (m/f) - My heart is at peace (especially when a dream comes true) (Obi). See also Obialọ

Obijiakụ (m) - A rich heart or the heart has the power of wealth (Obi)

Obi/m/na/efe/Chukwu (m) - My heart is worshipping God (Obi)

Obi/m/na/eto/ya (m) - My heart praises Him (God) or my heart is proud of him/her.

Obinna (m) - The Will (heart) of God (Obi)

ObiOlisa (m) - God's heart (a child or the beauty of God's heart is…) (Obi or Olisa)

Obiọma (m/f) - Kind-hearted (Obi)

Obiọra (m) - The good wish of the people (a community prayer/hope/ thoughts) (Obi). See also Nwọra

Obiụtọ (m) - Happiness or a glad heart (Obi)

Ọbụmneme (m) - It is not up to me (It's up to God) (Obum)

Ọbụmseluogo (m) - Did I cause the fight/war? (Obum or Obunse (Obunze))

Ọbunne (f) - Is it mother? Or it is mother (Nne)

Ọdiatụ (m) - The one I am proud of (Odi or Ody)

ỌdinakaChi or OdinakaChukwu (m) - It is in God's hands (Ody)

Ọfọdili (m) – 'A clear conscience fears no accusation.' See also Jideofor

Ogbenyeanụ (f) - A wish for a poor man not to be a suitor or husband

Ogbonnaya (m) - A son that has his father's resemblance or named after his father (Ogbo or Ogbonna). See also Enyinnaya

Ogo (f) - Blessing

OgeChikanma or OgeChukwuka (f) - God's time is the best (impeccable). (Oge or OgeChi)

ỌgoChukwu (f) - The grace (gift) of God (Ọgo)

Ọgomegbunam (m/f) - The hope that one's kindness should harm him/ her (Ogom)

Ọguejiọfọr (m) - Fight with a clear conscience (Ejiofor) See also Jideofor

Ọgugua (f/m) - The consoler or comforter

Ojiọfọr (m) - The one (anyone) who has a clear conscience

Okafor (m) – A male child born on 'Afor' market day

Ọkagbue (m) - To rebuke negativity (bad wish/energy or person)

Ọkadigbo (m) - It is still early for… (Kadi)

Ọkaomeh (m) - The one (anyone) who keeps to promise

OkeChi or OkeChukwu (m) - Share from God. (Okey)

Okeke (m) - A male child born on 'Eke' market day

Okolie or Okorie (m) - A male child born on 'Orie' market day

Okonkwọ (m) - A male child born on 'Nkwo' market day

Okwuadigbo (m) - A talk of (in) the past (regarding a past event) (Okwu)

OkwuChi (m/f) - The word of God

OkwudiliChukwu OkwudiliOlisa (m/f) - It's all (wishes/decisions) up to God. (Okwy, Okwii or Okwudili or Olisa (m))

Okwukwe (m/f) - Faith (Okwu or Okwii)

Okwuọma (f) - Good talk/sayings (Okwy or Okwii)

ỌlaChi (f) - Treasure of God (a child) (Ola)

Ọlaedo (f) - A treasured ornament (a treasured female child) (Ola)

Ọlanma (f) - A beautiful treasure (An ornament or a child) (Ola or Nma)

Olejuru (m/f) - Who can refuse this? (…a child or something good)

Olisadebe (m) – God stores/keeps… (Olisa)

Olisadera (f) - God has the final say (Dera). See also Chidera

Olisanugo (m) - God has heard (A plea for prayer, mercy…) (Olisa)

Olisaeloka (m) - God's thoughts are well-thought (The Will of God) (Olisa or Eloka)

Olisaemeka (m) - God has done marvelously. (Olisa, Emeka or Emy) See also Chukwuemeka and Nnaemeka

ỌlụChukwu (f) – The work of God (OluChi)

ỌmaChi (m/f) - He or she knows God or the blessings of God (it depends on the context of a situation) (Oma)

Ọmalicha (f) - Beauty or the beautiful one

Ọma/ta/oma/echi (Ọmataomaechi) (m) - If he/she knows today does he/ she know tomorrow? (Oma)

Omeokachie (m) - A man of his words. See also Ekwueme

Ọnaedo or Ọlaedo (f) - A treasure (priceless) (Ona or Ola)

Ọnochie (m) - The one who will replace another (after the death of a family member) of has replaced someone (or something) or basically, a male child that was born after the death of another male family member

ỌnụChukwu (m/f) - The mouth (word) of God

Ọnụora or Ọnuoha (m) - The mouth (wish) (Ọny)

Ọnwụamaegbu (m) - Death will not kill… (Onwu)

Ọnwụamaeze (m) - Death knows the royalty and the poor. Death does not discriminate between the rich and the poor

Ọnwụatuegwu (m) - Death is not afraid or I am not afraid of death (used differently depending on the context)

Ọnwụbiko (m) - A plea to death to please have mercy

Ọnwụdiwe (m) - Death is sadness or death depresses

Ọnwụghara (m) - Death, leave (us alone)

Ọnwụka (m) - Death is inevitable

Ọnwụemelie (m) - Death has won

Ọnwụmelu (m) - Death created this (sadness) condition and situation

OnyebụChi (m/f) - Who is (like) God? It is not really a question but, a connotation of man not being like God. (BuChi)

Onyediaso (m) - The Holy One

ỌnyedikaChi (m) - Who is like God? (Onyedika or Kaka)

ỌnyekaChi or ỌnyekaChukwu (m/f) - Who is greater than God? (Onyeka or KaChi)

Onyekaozulu (m) - Who has it all? It is simply a connotation that no one has it but, God. (Onyii) See also Ozuluonye.

OnyemaChukwu (m/f) - Who knows God? (Onyema or Onyii) See also AmaluChukwu.

Onyemaechi (m/f) – Who knows tomorrow? (Onyema or Onyii)

OnyemaucheChi or OnyemaucheChukwu (m/f) – Who knows God's mind (heart)? (Uche, UcheChi, Onyema, Onyi or Onyii)

Onyemere (m/f) - Who did? (A question posed when the impossible is done (a blessing) God)? (Onyii)

OnyenaChiya (m/f) – Destiny; literally means everyone with his/her God (same spirits in one God) (Onyii)

OnyeyiriChukwu (m) - Who resembles God! (Not really a question but, a symbol of the amazement of the goodness of God) (Onyeyiri)

OnyinyeChukwuka (m/f) - A gift from God is the greatest of all (Onyii or Onyinye).

Osadebe (m) See also Olisadebe

OsinaChi (m/f) - A gift (he/she as a gift or something) came from God (Osy, SinaChi or NaChi) See also IfesinaChi

Ositadimma or Tagbo (m) - (If) May things change positively from today then…it is a blessing (Ossy or Osita)

Ọsọndụ (m) - A flee for life (Ndụ)

Ọsụndụagwụike (m) - The run for life is never exhausting. Simply means that when is runs from death or harm, he/she runs tirelessly (Ọsondụ)

Otitodilinna or OtitodiliChukwu (m/f) - Glory be to God (Otito)

Oziọma (m/f) - Good news (Any type of good news or from the bible) (Ozi)

Ọzọemena (m/f) - The hope or wishes for bad events (death or accident) not repeat itself (Ozo)

Ozuluonye (m) - No one really has it all (Ozueh or Zulu). See also Onyekaozulu

R

RapụlụChukwu or RapụlụOlisa (m/f) - Commend it (everything) to God (Rapụlụ). See also HanyeChukwu

Rapụokwu (m) - Stop arguing (to avoid trouble)

Ralụeke (m) - Leave it up to the Creator (Ral)

S

SọChima (f) - Only God knows (SoChi or Chima)

SoChi (f) - Follow God

SolumtobeChukwu, SomkeneChukwu, SomtoChukwu or Somgolie (m/f) - Join me in praising God or rejoice with me (Somto, Solum, Somgoli, Kene or Tobe). See also Dumkene

Somadina (m/f) - A plea for companionship or simply saying; May I not be alone! (Soso, Soma or Dina)

SọpụlụChi or SọpụlụChukwu (m/f) - Respect God (Sọpụlụ)

T

ToChukwu, Tobenna or TobeOlisa (m/f) – Praise be to God or Praise God (Toby, To or Tobenna (m) or Tobe (m/f))

Toya (f) - Praise Him (God). See also EkenediliChukwu

U

Ụbanwa (m/f) - Ụba means wealth. Nwa means child. May our family's wealth richly through this child (Ụba)

UcheChukwu or Uchenna (m/f) - The mind/wishes (heart) of God (Uche or UcheChi). See also AmaucheChukwu

Udegbulam or Udegbunam (m) - May my kindness not harm me or backfire (UD or Ude). See also Ọgọmegbunam

Udobata (m/f) - May peace come (Ud)

Udokamma (m/f) - Peace is better (than disunity/war) (Udoka)

UgoChukwu or Ugonna (m/f) - The crown of God. 'Ugo' means an eagle; an eagle signifies beauty, royalty, purity, or excellence (UgoChi (f), Ugo (m) or U.G (f))

UgoChukwutubelum or Ugonnatubelum (m) - The crown (a gift of purity), God has given me, (Ugo, UgoChukwu or Ugonna). See also Adaugo

Ujunwa (f) - A child that came in peace (Uju). See also Obianuju

Ụkaegbulam or Ụkaegbunam (m) - May disagreement not kill me (Ụka or Egbuna)

Ụkamaka (f) - Good conversation (Uki or Amaka)

Ụlọma or Ụnọma (f) - Good home (Ụlọ/Ụnọ)

Urunna (m) - The value of a father (Uru)

Urunwa (f) - The value/rewards of a child. See also Nwamaka

Ụwaezuoke (m) - Literally means that even when you have earthly materials, your needs are still insatiable, No one has it all (Ụwa)

Ụwakwe (m) - The world needs to agree or If the world agrees…

Ụzọamaka, Ụzọdimma or Ụzọma (f) - The journey is a good one (Ụzọ or Amaka). See also Ijendụ or Ijeoma

ỤzoChi or ỤzọChukwu (m/f) - The path of God (Ụzọ)

Y

Yọbanna or YọbaChukwu (m/f) - Ask or beg God (YọbaChi)

Yanemezu (m) - He completes…'it' (Mezu)

Z

ZikọranaibụChim: Zikọra/na/ibụ/Chi/m (m/f) - Show the world that you are my God (Zikọra or IbụChim)

ZinaChidi or ZinaChukwudi (m/f) - Show that there is God (Zina (f), Chidi (m/f), Chuddy or Chụdi (m))

Zerenjo (f) - Avoid sin or evil (Zere)

Zereokwu (f) - Avoid enmity

Zikọra/na/Chi/di/mma or Zikọra/na/Chukwu/di/mma (m/f) - Show the world that God is good (Zikọra (m/f) or Chidinma (f))

Zikọra/na/udo/di/mma (m/f) - Show the world that peace is good (Zikọra or Udo, Udodi or Udodimma)

Zimụzọ (m) - Show me the way (Zim)

Zukọba (f) - Gather around (to celebrate) (Zukky)

To be African is a unique identity

Think About These For A Moment

- Imagine your life for a second. Is it imperfect? It is designed to be.
- You become what you assimilate into. Know the real you.
- Feed your mind with positive thoughts.
- Your heritage is your inheritance, therefore your right.
- Do more than exist and start living.
- Every good step you take is destined to be blessed, just like your every thought, but could be lost when misled.
- Your past should not determine nor deter your future. Life is all about choices.
- Behind your every smile and/or your every tear is the truth in your heart. Be true to yourself.
- Like a thief, jealousy lurks in the dark! In the end, jealousy does not pay. Who you are is who you should love. Be content with what you have.
- The storms of life can lock you down if you let it. Remember, you have the power to unlock your happiness, even through your pain.
- Life is a puzzle. Love is like a rose. Love is the journey of life. Live in love.
- The strength and the weakness of the heart depend on one's ability to choose defeat or victory!
- Ask yourself: Who am I without my name, my values? How did I get to where I am? How do I go to where I am destined to be?
- Remember, we are the reasons histories are made, so make your life a good story that would leave footprints in the halls of history.
- To achieve your goals, take the first step, and then, let God be God.

References

Generations of Igbos.

Okpala, Benneth Nnaedozie. Usoro Ihenkuzi Igbo: A Practical Approach to Teaching Igbo Language, Culture & Tradition.

The Holy Bible; King James Version.

http://www.learnigbonow.com

Http://www.newigbodictionary.com

Http://www.columbia.edu

Okolo, Don. 2007. Yeshua, My Love.

Anyanwu, Rose-Juliet. 1998. Aspects of Igbo Grammar. Phonetics, Phonology, Morphology, and the Tonology of Nouns. Hamburg: Lit Verlag.

Okolo, Don. 2010. Sodom City.